GHOSTS, HORROR AND HILLS

Where folklore and eerie mists linger

ADITYA KANT

Vitasta

Published by
Vitasta Publishing Pvt Ltd
C-29, Sector-7, Noida, Uttar Pradesh - 201301
info@vitastapublishing.com

ISBN: 978-93-47098-79-6

First Edition 2025
Reprint 2026

MRP ₹395

Edited by Reena Singh

Typeset by Shubhpreet Kaur

Cover Design by Rohit Gautam

Printed by Manipal Technologies Limited, Manipal

'Aditya Kant's plot conception is deep, unpredictable, and it hits you with a bang. His small chapters, often like sharp missiles, never miss their target. His prose is rooted in Himachali culture, yet expressed in his impeccable English and effortless flow. When access to fiction is tuned with years of journalism and a rare cinematic eye, a certain magic emanates. I look forward to anything written by him.'

-Rajan Khosa (BAFTA voting member, writer, and director of films like 'Gattu' and 'Dance of the Wind')

'Ghosts are all around us. Look for them, and you will find them.'

— Ruskin Bond

Dedicated to my parents and
to the Kant family

CONTENTS

FOREWORD

Migrating from one style of writing to another is one of the most difficult tasks. It demands self-discipline, motivation, and mental energy. Yet Aditya Kant has managed the transition with ease.

His journey from journalistic writing to the domain of fiction has been both eventful and a testament to perseverance. Choosing the hills as a backdrop to write fiction came naturally to him. Born and raised in Himachal Pradesh, he has always carried the rhythms of the mountains within him. Even though his professional compulsions took him to the plains of Delhi and Chandigarh and the arid and semi-arid landscapes of Rajasthan and Gujarat, the call of the hills never left him.

His plunge into the world of horror and the supernatural also feels organic. He belongs to a generation for whom ghosts have always been a part of growing up and fuel for their imagination. Not literally, but incidents and anecdotes linked to the supernatural phenomena were woven into the daily life of his generation. It was rare for a day to pass without some reference to spirits, or some inexplainable happenings.

Those were the times when the hill towns were sparsely populated and homes located far apart from each other. Forests lay close by and the rustling of leaves and swishing sounds of the flora was an everyday soundtrack. One just needed a bit of imagination amid ample time at hand to feel the wilderness, calm, interplay of the moon and the clouds.

Those were heady days when life thrived away from the screen, be it that of television or mobile phones. Aditya Kant captures those moments of a bygone era in his stories, whether describing the locales of Shimla, Kullu, Dharamshala or other hill towns or hamlets.

It is perhaps only the hill folk who can understand the loneliness embodied in characters such as Baba Yaga, the famous witch of Russian literature. In Himachal Pradesh, there are several such characters that lived in folklore and conversation.

Aditya Kant has penned down the tales that remind one of the times when such stories were shared by friends and cousins in the past as they cuddled together in their quilts in the harsh winters with no power supply at times, moving from small talk to stories of ghosts and witches. The wide-eyed expressions on the face of the listeners at the end of the session told their own tale. Quite often, they would refuse to sleep alone or even go to the neighbouring house without company.

This is the essence that Aditya Kant has captured in his stories. His style of writing is musical and rhythmic like the pace of life in the hills. The most important aspect of his writing is the ability to convey the message without using bombastic language. His language is simple, clear, and inviting, making his stories accessible to readers who seek an easy, engaging read. Such books are crucial for drawing the attention of first-time readers, helping to sustain the art of reading itself, now increasingly confined to a smaller circle.

If ghosts can inspire a person to pick up a book, what is the harm? His stories also capture the subtle details of local culture, beliefs, and practices. Those who have lived in the hills will find themselves immediately connected to the plots of his stories, while those who are new to hill life will discover much to reflect upon.

Come to think of it, the hills still retain buildings that have been considered haunted for decades. Families still warn children to keep away from certain spots. Occultism is very much alive in villages. On days people avoid from venturing out after dark, and thorny hedges are placed at their doorsteps to ward off evil spirits from entering their abodes.

Aditya Kant has lived in this milieu and it is reflected

in his short stories with authenticity and power. It is easy to connect with the supernatural. As you turn the pages, it feels as if the ghosts are sitting right beside you, reading.

Cheers
Rajeev Khanna
First Reader, Senior Journalist and Critic

PREFACE

There was a time when the hills lulled us to sleep with bedtime stories whispered by grannies, mothers, and elders. Life moved at a far gentler pace back then, untouched by mobile phones, social media, and even television. Books were treasured companions, and the chilling thrill of ghost stories shared during school lunch breaks or before sunset walks home brought haunting euphoria. With fewer distractions and more room for imagination, our surroundings took on deeper meaning and even deeper mysteries.

Growing up in the quiet townships of Solan, Mandi, Kullu, and Sujanpur Tihra (Hamirpur), and later in the nostalgic embrace of the erstwhile British Capital of Shimla, I lived through countless ghostly tales and supposed paranormal encounters.

In the seventies, eighties, and early nineties, such stories were not merely fiction; they were part of communal folklore. They echoed through tea shops, classrooms, hostels and social gatherings, passed down from friends to cousins to strangers with such conviction that they were hard to dismiss. In those quieter times, being the youngest of four siblings made me an easy target for ghostly pranks, but it also infused in me a vivid love for the eerie and the unexplained.

These spectral tales were never just about fear; they were about imagination, curiosity, and bonding. Whether it was summoning spirits at midnight in the hostel rooms or sensing an eerie presence along a snow-laden path from Chaura Maidan to Summer Hill in Shimla, the haunted landscape of the hills offered more than scenic beauty. It offered an atmosphere ripe for scary stories.

With the new millennium came the digital deluge. Mobile phones, reels, and WhatsApp messages began to replace whispered tales and shared chills. The mountains, though still serene and beautiful, started ringing more with notification pings than spine-tingling stories. Yet the memories, the stories, and the ghosts never truly left me.

The idea of writing these spooky stories struck me about fifteen years ago after a conversation with my friend Saurabh Malik, himself an ardent ghost-story enthusiast. I even began working on some of these stories but took a break to focus on my debut novel *High on Kasol.* Even so, the spirits of those stories kept calling me back.

This collection is more than a series of ghost stories. It

brings together nineteen spine-chilling fictional accounts set in contemporary times against the picturesque yet eerie backdrop of Himachal Pradesh. Some stories unfold in well-known towns while others explore lesser-known places and villages. They weave local legends, paranormal encounters, and the unsettling shadows of recent events, into narratives that bridge the mystical with the contemporary.

My heartfelt gratitude goes to the young Highlanders family—Triveni, Archit, Damini, Arjit, Swastik, Amogh, Akshiti, Tarush, Maatangi, Mridul, Aditi, Aurnav, Tejaswini, Abhiraj, Yugank, and Swapnil—whose laughter and shivers during our late-night storytelling sessions encouraged me to keep writing. This book is also for Gen Z, including my daughter Ananya, who, despite the pull of social media, remains curious about the imaginary shadows that linger outside the windows of her room, when the wind blows at midnight.

My deepest thanks to my editors Cora Bhatia, for polishing and making my stories crisper and Reena Singh for her unwavering belief in my voice; my blunt and honest first reader, Rajeev Khanna; my wife, Seema whose encouragement and own spooky childhood tales breathed life into some of these stories; Arvind Sharma and Shanti Swaroop whose belief in my storytelling never wavered, and to Deepan Joshi, a gifted and imaginative storyteller, whose sudden departure left us with fond memories of his heartwarming stories. A special note of gratitude to former colleague and friend Manish Choure for his brilliant inputs and suggestions for the title and design of the book.

My sincere appreciation goes to Renu Kaul Verma for believing in this collection of ghost stories and the entire team of Vitasta Publishing for their support.

Crafting these ghost stories has been a journey through memories and imagination. The genesis of this collection lies in my childhood. In those days, there were no multiplexes or streaming platforms. Stories were passed along like treasured secrets while the silver screen retained its unique magic.

My heartfelt thanks to some of my primary school classmates, especially my childhood friend, Rakesh Bodh.

He holds a special place in acknowledgments, being among my earliest and most dedicated listeners for several fictional tales I would invent, often presenting them as real incidents.

I vividly remember the cold, wintry afternoons, when gathered around the *angeethi*, we would recount scary stories of horror films during our school lunch breaks. We would painstakingly craft special sound effects using our only voices, to capture our small audience's attention.

Perhaps, those were the days, when my fascination with the spectral and the art of spinning chilling stories first took root.

Finally, this book wouldn't be what it is without my alma mater, Sainik School Sujanpur Tihra. Growing up in the foothills of the Dhauladhar Range, not far from the enduring flow of the mighty Beas, was to me, far more than textbooks. It was about mastering the art of storytelling, forging friendships on the football field, and developing a sixth sense for spotting hostel warden patrols. Looking back, these skills turned out far more useful than the mind-bending riddles of trigonometry and mathematical equations.

A huge shoutout to my classmates and roommates, the brave souls who welcomed my fictional tales and lost Bollywood plots with the reverence usually reserved for legends. They made storytelling an adventure long before I realised what I was doing.

Finally, my heartfelt appreciation to the readers who embraced *High on Kasol.* Your love and encouragement inspired me to return with this collection. I hope these stories carry you back to a time when fear had a face, mystery, a voice, and our imaginations walked besides us, with ghosts lurking in the snow, whispering by a gurgling river, or hiding behind the old wooden panels of a cupboard.

A WHISPER OF CAUTION!

As you begin reading, I can imagine the pages turning on their own…and a husky voice rising from behind the curtain's shadows, whispering a warning in a hushed tone: 'Don't leave a story half way. Read it to the end or I will start reading it aloud to you!'

No need to turn around.

Wishing you a happy haunting reading!

SHUDDERING HEIGHTS

'Now I know what a ghost is. Unfinished business, that's what.'

—Salman Rushdie

It was just another day of the peak tourist season in the Solang valley, about twenty-four kilometres from Manali. Yet, for the past few days, this favourite hub of fun-loving tourists and adventure-seekers had lost some of its allure due to continuous rain and threatening overcast skies.

Raju Thakur was optimistically examining the wings and harness of his paraglider, ensuring everything was ready to take off as soon as the weather cleared. The harness, speed bar, and the brakes looked secure and properly connected to the wing fluttering in the gusty wind.

He had become extra cautious about safety measures after the accidental death of a paraglider over a year ago. The young tourist had fallen, together with his instructor, after their harness developed a snag. Since then, the local administration too had increased vigilance and were conducting frequent surprise checks to prevent such accidents from recurring.

Always a perfectionist, Raju wanted everything to be in perfect order.

Originally a travel agent in Manali, he had trained to become a certified instructor for paragliding. Taking advantage of a small tours and travel start-up in Manali, he had expanded into adventure sports.

Along with his business partner, Sherry Bragta, he managed a small team of youngsters who organised trekking, mountaineering, and paragliding activities in the valley. An adventure lover himself, Raju was fond of paragliding and enjoyed flying through the sky, often accompanied by thrill-seekers eager to indulge their adrenaline cravings.

Solang Valley, the renowned adventure hub of Himachal, nestled at a height of over 8,500 feet, offered plenty of opportunities for such pursuits.

Observing adventure-seekers, particularly novices—embarking on their flights amused and fascinated Raju. Many youngsters expressed their fears and excitement in shrill voices, while others, especially new couples pretended to be cool at take-off, but quickly lost composure mid-flight once they saw how high they were above the mountains and river below. They would beg for an early landing.

A recent video, shot mid-air had gone viral. It featured a smartly dressed corporate executive from Noida pleading with Raju to ensure a safe landing while Raju rebuked him for not following the instructions carefully. The video had made Raju one of the best-known faces amongst the certified instructors in the area.

The fleeting panic just before lift-off, the occasional uncertainty during the glide through the sky and the exultation or simple relief on landing—all made for a fascinating glimpse into human nature.

'Hey, are you open for the day? Will you be taking flights?' a sweet voice interrupted Raju's train of thought.

She stood there sporting sky-blue jeans and a white top, with matching blue-and-white sneakers. She appeared to be in her early twenties; she carried a small handbag in her henna-stained hands and wore a tiny gold ring on one finger.

'I am Niharika,' she said, holding back the silky brown hair that fluttered in the breeze. 'I just can't wait to take to the skies.'

She ran her slender, tapering fingers along the smooth polyester of the wing. 'How's the wind today?'

Raju looked meaningfully at her for a while before replying, 'Terrific!'

He wanted to compliment her further but hesitated, mindful of the vermillion streak in her parting and the *bindi* on her forehead, which hinted at her marital status.

'Listen!' she continued eagerly. 'I need to take this flight. Will you take me high up in the sky? I need to give my hubby a big, *big* surprise!'

Her bubbling enthusiasm and persuasive tone made her appeal irresistible, especially because she seemed to reciprocate his mild flirtation.

Swallowing hard, Raju finally found his words. 'Ma'am, you'll have to wait a little while. Let the wind settle down a bit. We can't take any risks,' he said earnestly, unable to look away from her bright kohled eyes.

In truth, he was eager to take the sortie. Everything was inspected; the equipment was in order. He was eager to glide on the wind towards the sun, which peeked uncertainly from behind white and grey clouds. It was a promising sign for a flight.

'It's our fifth wedding anniversary,' she continued, unperturbed. 'You see that white car there outside the café?'

She pointed towards a canopy over the open-air eatery in the distance, where tourists sat enjoying snacks and drinks.

'I want to give my husband a spectacular view. He thinks I'm too timid for the sky.'

She paused and added brightly, 'Actually, we had a funny outing the last time when we visited here for our honeymoon.'

She pulled out her mobile and showed Raju a video.

'That was quite a scene I created mid-air! I really made a fool of myself.'

What she showed him was nothing unusual for him. He had seen several tourists panic before and during their take-off. Niharika had behaved no differently. She was almost in tears, reluctant as a child before stepping onto the launch pad, mouthing words angrily at her husband, who could not be seen in the video, but could be heard laughing loudly in the background.

Raju did not bother to watch the video and cut her short. 'That's fine, Ma'am. Once the winds settle, you will be the first to go,' he said scanning the scattered clouds overhead.

'The wind has slowed down,' she persisted. 'It's not even drizzling. It will be clear by the time you seat me in the harness.'

She seemed in no mood to relent.

Raju knew it was time to prepare for the flight.

'First, you need to tie up your hair—it's long and beautiful, if you don't mind me saying so—and tuck it under the helmet,' he instructed, handing her the safety gear.

He loosely positioned himself under the wing behind her and showed her how to buckle herself to the harness securely. After adjusting the brakes and confirming everything was correctly in place,' he decided that Niharika and he were ready to fly in tandem.

As they began the short run-up, Raju stole a glimpse of the talkative woman's face. It had turned pale and stern. She had stopped her constant chatter. Smiling to himself, he began giving instructions for the takeoff.

'Just focus! Take a deep breath. We're about to jump soon.'

'I'm going blank,' she managed to shout back. 'I'm not scared of dying... but still... do you think I'll be able to do this and land back safely?'

'Don't worry, ma'am. I do more than twenty such flights daily. Nothing will happen to you,' he assured her firmly, performing the manoeuvres, as the wing was raised at the apex directly above them. They went into a controlled and progressive run in the direction of the wind.

In his five years as a pilot, Raju had experienced a near-accident only once when a woman had a panic attack in the sky. She had begun crying as the wind suddenly grew in stronger, lifting their paraglider to such a height that they could not land for nearly an hour.

But that was an exceptional case. Now, Niharika and he jumped neatly off the cliff and the wind lifted them upwards. Raju could hear her murmuring something. 'Are you okay, Ma'am?' he asked.

He saw her barely nod.

'Just look at the clouds!' he urged her. 'Imagine you are one of them—or pretend to be an angel! Later, you can show your husband that you were not scared at all. I am recording everything on this camera. Look up, to your right. Say something—anything—to your hubby.'

They both smiled, and Raju clicked a still from the video recording. 'Don't you worry,' he reassured her once more. I'm recording the entire flight.'

Niharika calmed down and no longer appeared nervous or for that matter, even excited.

'Yes,' she resumed in a conversational tone. 'It took me a hell of a lot of courage to come up here, but I'm not scared at all.'

Then, to Raju's surprise she added, 'In fact, I have *never* been afraid of death.'

Raju wondered what had suddenly come over her but said nothing.

'I can ride the clouds on my own, you know,' she continued, 'I don't need all this to be in the clouds.'

'But you wanted to prove a point to your hubby, right?' Raju asked, feeling a bit jittery.

'Hubby? My foot! He's no longer with me. He married my best friend and is now enjoying his honeymoon,' she said, her girlish voice suddenly faltering.

Raju heard her break into louder and louder laughter, which only stopped when she commanded him hoarsely over the wind, '*Come on*, give me the controls. Let *me* handle this!' She snatched control of the brake and speed handles from Raju, whose turn it was now to be gripped by fear.

Niharika began to tamper with the risers and pressed her feet onto the speed bar. They passed through turbulence and started to gain altitude. But she showed no sign of stopping.

'*Ma'am, we're going above the prescribed height!*' Raju warned. 'The winds are too strong at this altitude, and we could be blown away!'

'Let it be!' she screamed. '*I* am not afraid. Let me show *you* some stunts.'

Fiddling with the risers, she made the glider zigzag through the air.

'Ma'am!' Raju roared, nearly into her ear. 'We're going to die! *Please give back* the control,' he pleaded as they soared higher and higher.

But nothing worked on her, neither shouts nor recriminations.

'Tell my hubby he's a cheat and a murderer,' she said calmly. 'He tampered with the paraglider's suspensions that caused the accident last time. He killed me.'

Before Raju could respond, she cackled again, 'But good riddance to bad rubbish. Who the hell wants to live with *him?*'

Suddenly, one of the safety straps snapped. They swung sharply to their left, losing altitude in a sickening lurch. It felt like a free fall. The wind whistled in their ears, but not loud enough to drown the sound of her laughter.

Raju desperately tried to apply the brakes, managing only to slow their downward swoop.

The sky spun around him. Moments later, they hit the ground with a thud. He thought he heard voices approaching, but everything went black.

Sometime later, Raju woke up in a moving vehicle. The screaming siren told him it was an ambulance. Excruciating pain seared in his legs and spine. As he opened his eyes, he saw his partner Sherry holding him still.

'Don't try to move,' Sherry warned anxiously. 'You have multiple fractures, but thank heavens you're alive!'

Raju stared at Sherry blankly.

'What happened to you?' Sherry looked even more concerned, as if Raju had lost his mind. 'Why did you suddenly take off on a flight without telling me? And in this weather? Couldn't you have waited for the winds to settle?'

'I w-w-anted to but she w-w-ouldn't listen,' Raju stuttered in a whisper.

'H-h-ow's she doing, anyway?'

'Who? What are you talking about? You were *alone*! You went on a flight *on your own!* You took a *solo* flight,' Sherry sounded as if he was explaining things to a dopehead.

Raju was even more confused. 'There's nothing wrong with me,' he said, irritated. 'I went ahead because she insisted.'

Then, to avoid admitting he had been beguiled by her charms, he added: 'Sh-sh-she even offered me double the amount.'

He fumbled awkwardly in his chest pocket for his mobile, relieved to find it was intact.

'Let me show you the video.'

Raju played the recording. His voice could be heard

saying, 'Hello, Ma'am, see, I'm recording it.'

But the footage showed only him in the sky surrounded by white floating clouds, talking to no one. She wasn't there.

'You must be hallucinating. Stop sneaking a joint first thing in the morning or you will die one day in the sky,' Sherry said disgusted and disbelieving.

A sudden thought pierced through Raju's foggy mind. He grabbed his mobile again and googled randomly on it. *Niharika … tourist … Paragliding…*

A news report popped up:

24 June, Manali: *Niharika Rathore, 24, a newly married tourist from Jaisalmer and her pilot Jhabe Ram, 34 are suspected to have met with a paragliding accident near Dhobi village, a few kilometres from the Solang valley. Locals awaiting them on the ground believe freakish winds prevented them from landing at the expected position and carried them away higher in the mountains. However, neither of the bodies have yet been found. The authorities have stepped up search and rescue operations.*

Raju was speechless. Frustration and pain overwhelmed him and caused him to pass out again. He didn't register when the stretcher-bearers lifted him and carried him into the hospital.

***

A few hours later, he lay trussed up in a surgical bed, both legs encased in plaster. Sherry stood beside him, holding his hand, tears brimming in his eyes.

Raju longed to console his partner. 'Believe me, bro! I didn't go solo. That woman persuaded me to take her. But once we were in the air, she took over and caused this accident.'

But Sherry's woebegone eyes didn't even flicker in response.

'He can't hear you,' said a familiar voice sweetly from the other side of his bed.

'No one can.'

Raju turned his eyes towards the speaker—a nurse in a crisp white pinafore and neatly pinned cap. He saw her long brown hair, framed kohled eyes and an infectious smile he had remembered so well. He rubbed his eyes, trying to clear them and recognised Niharika. She was beckoning him with those elegant fingers he'd found so captivating.

'Come,' she said silkily. 'We have an unfinished task to complete. My hubby's all kitted up and ready to paraglide. Let's scare him to death!' She flashed another of her irresistible smiles.

The agonising pain was gone. Raju stood up effortlessly.

Hand in hand, they walked through the door.

Raju turned back once. Sherry had buried his face in his hands, silent in grief.

On the bed lay Raju's motionless body. His plastered legs hung with heavy weights. His eyes remained wide open, fixed on the open doorway.

The monitor beside him showed a thin, straight line. Silent.

MISSED CALL

'She thought love had returned. But it was only grief wearing his face.'

The year was 2008 and it was Christmas Eve in Shimla. The narrow lanes between stalls laden with festive goods were jammed to capacity with tourists thronging to the hill town dreaming of a white Christmas. Peehu battled her way through Lakkar Bazaar, hurrying to reach Chaura Maidan, which was still half an hour away if she didn't speed up.

She was meeting her old friend, Ateet who was in town on another one of his lightning visits. He had secured admission to the Department of Indian Theatre at Panjab University in Chandigarh and had recently moved there. As a result, their meetings had become less frequent. Peehu had stayed behind in Shimla, pursuing her Masters in English from Himachal Pradesh University. She lived in one of the girl's hostels at Summer Hill. During college days, they would meet after lectures at a rain shelter in Chaura Maidan and spend hours chatting, at a nearby tea-stall in the sun. Now they saw each other only once every three or four months when Ateet visited his parents in Shimla. Every minute together was precious.

Ateet usually arrived in the evenings. As soon as he alighted at 103 Tunnel, a bus stop named after the nearby railway tunnel, he would call Peehu and dash to the rain shed to meet her. His last message to Peehu indicated he would arrive around 6.30 pm.

A happy-go-lucky guy, Ateet dreamed of making it big in Bollywood. He often mimicked top Bollywood heroes and villains, sharing anecdotes about his small interactions with them. During college, he had worked as a junior artiste in some movies shot on location and took pride in showing her the footage.

Their tea sessions would continue until the alarm on Peehu's mobile beeped reminding her of her 8 pm deadline to return to the hostel. The warden was a strict curfew-keeper and would not allow inmates to enter the premises after 9 pm. Ateet would always accompany Peehu on the lonely stretch from Chaura Maidan to her hostel because she feared walking alone, especially in the evenings, when the thick forest of deodars loomed over them.

Ateet loved teasing her with spooky tales of ghosts around Summer Hill, claiming that long-dead inhabitants of the once British summer capital haunted their old homes.

The most-often narrated incident was of a white-faced stranger in a long overcoat who had appeared out of nowhere in the middle of the road at night and stretched out an arm asking for a matchbox from a solitary walker. A theatre enthusiast and a freshly enrolled student of drama, Ateet would add a wide variety of sound effects to his enactments—including the English accent of the intruding ghosts—evoking nervous giggles from Peehu.

Recalling their last outing, Peehu hurried past the Kali Bari temple since the rain shelter was still about a kilometre away. She was already late. Her mobile showed it was already 6.30 pm, and Ateet, who disliked waiting, would likely be annoyed.

'It's better to apologise well in advance,' she muttered to herself as she dialled Ateet's number.

But the call went unheard or at least, unanswered.

She slipped her mobile back in the leather bag, swung it over her fragile shoulders, and quickened her pace until she finally reached the rain shed.

As expected, Ateet was already there, looking effortlessly cool in his favourite slim-fit light blue jeans and a long black jacket with a hood. He had lit a cigarette and squinted against the smoke, searching for her through the dwindling crowd of passengers.

'Sorry Mr Punctual!' Peehu said breezily, trying to laugh away his irritation. 'I got late again. Lakkar Bazar was crowded. I promise this is the last time.'

'Look, I tried to call you but you didn't pick up,' she added apologetically.

Ateet, happy merely to see her, didn't bother to argue.

'Fine! Last time, yeah! I too promise this is the last one,' he smiled and ground out the half-burnt butt of the cigarette under his heel. It was a vow often made whenever Peehu objected to his smoking, citing the habit's dangers.

He quickly changed the subject this time. 'Let's grab a cup of tea before Pandeyji calls it a day,' he suggested, looking towards the old tea-stall owner, whom they had seen running the shop since childhood.

Ateet's drama classes were going well and he was learning the art of modulating voices. He had recently scored the highest marks in an assessment where students had to imitate any animal of their choosing. That was his latest update from his theatre classes for Peehu.

'So, what animal did you choose?' Peehu asked, grinning as she finished her tea.

'A lazy crocodile basking in the sun by the riverside doing nothing but waiting for its prey. All I had to do was move my eyes, while lying still on my abdomen,' he said, rolling his big eyeballs in a circle, clockwise and then anti-clockwise.

'You must have scared the hell out of them,' Peehu said mockingly, although she had always admired the intensity of his gaze when he was pretending to be someone or something else.

Soon her 8 pm alarm began to beep on the mobile.

'I need to make a dash for it,' said Peehu in a panic,

fumbling for a twenty-rupee note in her purse and handing it to Pandeyji. 'I don't fancy being locked out in the dark night by the dragon lady.'

As usual, Ateet escorted her to her hostel. Nothing stirred in the night air except a firefly, which he pointed out in the bushes. 'Oh! Look there!' he cried in excitement. 'Mr Johnson has finally found the match to light his cigarette with!'

That was enough to startle Peehu. She screamed and grabbed Ateet's arm tightly. Anticipating her reaction, Ateet pulled her close to him and gave a mischievous smile with a wink.

'Thank you, gentleman!' he bowed grandly to an unseen figure. 'I owe you a lighter and a full pack of cigarettes,' he declared, turning towards the bushes and bursting into laughter.

Realising that it was a prank, Peehu mock punched his broad shoulders with her delicate fists in protest. Then she relented and joined in his laughter.

They were approaching the Summer Hill bus stop. Her hostel was barely a few hundred metres away.

'I can go on my own from here,' Peehu said firmly. 'You go ahead and spend time with your parents. Tomorrow is Christmas, remember? We'll have the whole day together!' She waved an excited goodbye.

Ateet waved back reluctantly but said nothing.

She had walked only a few metres further when the

mobile in her purse started to ring. Still running towards her hostel, she fumbled to take it out. Ateet's number flashed on the screen.

'Oh no! Now what? Why can't he stop playacting for once?' she muttered angrily and disconnected the call.

She was already late and dreaded the scolding she was likely to receive from the warden at the entrance.

But the mobile rang again. This time she answered, irritated.

'Stop your theatrics, Ateet! Let me get to my room at least,' she snapped.

'Ma'am! Don't hang up, please!'

It was not Ateet.

'Madam! This is Sub-Inspector Tek Chand from Shoghi Police Post.

'There was a massive landslide earlier this evening. A bus from Chandigarh fell into the gorge just before the hairpin turn towards Shimla.

'There are several casualties. The rescue team found your number on the 'missed call' list of someone's mobile lying on the hillside. Can you come and identify the owner?' the caller asked urgently.

Peehu looked wordlessly back towards the Summer Hill bus stop, still hoping this was just another of Ateet's dramatics. But he was nowhere to be seen even in the distance.

'Ma'am! Are you there? You can accompany one of

the rescue teams that are arriving from your area,' the caller urged her. The shocking news left her numb and disoriented. Her heart, was in no state to grasp or accept the harsh reality, cycling as it was through denial and disbelief.

'This can't be true. He was just here and we were laughing,' she uttered disbelievingly, clinging to the last memory of him.

Soon a blaring PCR van arrived and a policeman approached her. 'Madam, please come with me and help us identify the victim.'

She followed him blindly and sat in the van, her mind a storm of fragmented thoughts and images, a chaotic jumble reflecting the sudden and violent disruption of her reality. The familiar hills outside the van now seemed alien, triggering fresh waves of emotions. The rain shed and the tea stall they had visited together so often appeared like ghosts of happier times, intensifying the pain of Ateet's absence.

Throughout the journey a deep sense of emptiness and longing consumed her. She did not realise when the officer accompanying her ushered her to the accident spot.

'He is in his mid-twenties, fair-complexioned, around five foot eight, wearing light blue jeans and a black-hooded jacket.'

His voice sounded like a death knell amid the blaring sirens of the ambulances. A crushing wave of intense grief and sorrow engulfed her.

Peehu stood frozen as a stone, staring down at the still body of the exuberant friend she'd just spent an entire evening with, who had not been able to take her call and whose bus hadn't even made it to the 103 Tunnel bus stop in Shimla.

Her best friend and would be companion had parted ways, but not before keeping his promise to meet her. It was the beginning of a long and arduous journey through the landscape of grief; one Peehu would now traverse with only memories of Ateet.

THE BREATHLESS ATTENDANT

'He died with his hand still holding a mask—and now he moves unseen, adjusting drips, whispering words of peace, standing watch when no one else can.'

The clock struck two in the morning in the Intensive Care Unit (ICU) of Sundarpur Hospital. The main lights had been extinguished, leaving only the dim flicker of a tube light in the corner. Most patients lay motionless in their beds, their shapes indistinguishable from the shadows. The newly built Covid Hospital nestling in the foothills of the Himalayas pulsed with an unsettling silence. Only the occasional, rhythmic beeping of monitors and the ragged, desperate wheeze of patients tethered to oxygen masks, broke the silence, which echoed in the overcrowded ward of the Intensive Care Unit.

The second wave of Covid had ravaged the region. The hospital's corridors, wards, and the already overburdened 22-bed ICU were now overflowing with the hapless sufferers suspended between life and death.

Forty-year-old Abhi Verma lay on a stretcher in a corner, struggling to steady his breathing, while keeping an eye at the monitor beside him. The day had been long and brutal; he had been rushed here after his oxygen levels plummeted to a dangerous 75 per cent. Now, with the virus affecting his lungs, the next twenty-fours hours were critical. The X-ray and MRI scans confirmed the infection in his lungs was spreading to a dangerous level

As Abhi was finally admitted to the ICU, he witnessed the haunting reality of the pandemic. A frantic son used an Ambu bag to help his dying father breathe. His life slipped away, despite his son's desperate attempts.

Outside in the corridor, the dead were piled up on stretchers and trolleys. The class IV medical staff of the hospital had packed the bodies for a quick and unceremonious cremation in a nearby makeshift crematorium. Families were not permitted inside. Instead, they waited silently outside in a hall, staring through the glass at their loved ones one last time.

Abhi was allotted bed Number 7, vacated just an hour earlier after its previous occupant's demise. He clipped the pulse oximeter to his finger and watched as the infrared light slowly appeared, showing his oxygen level at ninety. Still below normal, but at least not falling further. His pulse was steady at seventy-four.

Relieved, Abhi removed his mask for a moment, trying to ease the suffocating claustrophobia it caused him. The thin green strap had been digging into his skin, leaving a mark behind his ears. He turned off the oxygen valve behind his bed and looked around the dimly lit room. A dozen patients lay scattered in the shadowy stillness; each locked in their own battle against the deadly virus.

In the far-left corner, an elderly man coughed uncontrollably, each spasm causing him to gasp for breath while desperately trying to remove the oxygen mask from his bearded face in futile attempts to ease his suffering.

'Are you in a hurry to die? Why are you removing your mask? What was the need to come and crowd the hospital if you did not want to survive?' the senior nurse scolded the man, while fixing her mask yet again. The burden of tending to the overwhelming flow of patients was etched on her face.

The bearded man only raised his hands mockingly as though accustomed to her scoldings. When she moved on to the other patients, he resumed tugging at his mask, stubborn as ever.

To Abhi's left was an overweight middle-aged woman, breathing heavily. The nurse had given her some medicines and injections to steady her blood pressure; Abhi had overheard the staff whispering that the woman was critical and might not make it through the night. But her suffering had not deterred the woman from frequently smiling at Abhi. Shortly after Abhi's arrival, she had asked about his health and told him that she too had a son, who was an engineering student in Bangalore. Abhi had seen her make a video call to him, a few moments before her breathing had worsened due to the combined effect of Covid and her rising blood pressure.

A teenage boy nearby was lost in his mobile phone. He filled the room with frequent giggles as awkward laughter emanated from some of the reels he was watching. He seemed oblivious to the grim reality around him.

On the other side of Abhi's bed, an aged man, was preparing for discharge in the morning. Abhi had overheard the staff marvel at his recovery, despite his age. It was a rare moment of hope amidst a sea of worsening conditions. Amid all this, Abhi's hope flickered dimly as he battled to stay conscious; every moment seemed a struggle against the encroaching darkness. His gaze fixed helplessly on the wall clock above the entrance, its hands crawling lethargically. The hour hand crept forward with excruciating slowness, each tick of the minute hand a torturous echo in the silence. Dawn was far away; it was only 2.30 am.

The nursing staff had gone a while ago, leaving only the suffering and the darkness behind.

The ICU's tube light flickered ominously, casting eerie shadows. The monotonous beeping of monitors and the low hum of exhaust fans filled the deafening silence.

Suddenly, a loud thud shattered the stillness. A woman's anguished cries pierced the night. 'Oh God, someone help me! I've broken my back! I can't get up!'

The middle-aged woman from the adjacent bed had fallen on the floor. Her voice was laced with pain and desperation as she writhed on the floor, her oxygen pipes severed, her breathing growing more ragged with each moment.

Abhi's heart raced as he realised he could not move much due to the canola in his arm. He was too weak to lift her back onto the bed, and there was no one to help—the corridors outside were filled with waiting patients, their faces masked by the darkness.

'Someone help! Please! Is anyone there?' Abhi shouted, panic rising in his chest. But only the mournful beep of monitors and the hum of the fans answered him.

'Don't waste your time. Come with me. Let's help her!' A baritone voice cut through the gloom.

Abhi turned to see the bearded man from the extreme left corner, the one who had been scolded earlier for removing his mask. Despite his own distress, the man's smile was unsettling—a fixed, strange grin that did not reach his eyes.

'Sir, you took off your oxygen mask again?' Abhi asked, his voice trembling.

'Don't worry about that. Let's just help her,' the man replied with an eerie calm.

Together, they approached the woman. The bearded man took her feet while Abhi supported her back and head. With great effort, they lifted her back onto the bed and the bearded man restored her oxygen mask, ensuring the flow was steady.

'Now you should rest and put your mask back on, young man,' the bearded man instructed in his deep, resonant voice before turning toward the ICU's exit.

Abhi, still shaken, watched the bearded man, heading towards the restroom. He put on his oxygen mask and soon fell into an uneasy sleep.

At dawn, the rattling of a stretcher jolted him awake. Attendants had surrounded the bearded man's bed in the corner. The monitor had been moved, and they were setting up a screen around him.

'What's happening?' Abhi asked weakly.

The head nurse looked at him, her face grim. 'The man passed away last night. His mask was found removed.'

'What? When did this happen? He helped me lift the woman when she fell from the bed last night?' Abhi uttered disbelievingly.

'The monitor shows his heart stopped beating around 2 am,' the nurse told him indifferently.

Abhi's blood ran cold. The realisation hit him: the bearded man had helped him lift the woman almost half an hour after he had passed away.

The horror of the ICU settled in Abhi's heart as he lay back, shivering. The bearded man's final, haunting smile replayed in his mind and he put on his oxygen mask, wondering if anyone would believe him. He looked at the overweight woman by his side, who had fallen from the bed the preceding night. She too was looking at him disbelievingly.

THE SURVIVOR AND THE DEAD

'The last man on Earth sat alone in a room.
There was a knock on the door…'

—Fredric Brown, *Knock*

October seemed the perfect time to venture out into the hills once more. After two years of near-confinement in their home, in Chandigarh, photographer Shaurya Veer and his family were finally breaking some of the bonds that the Covid epidemic had imposed on them. Their excitement was immense. The thrill was doubled because they were making the trip in their new SUV—a gift Shaurya and his wife Mona had indulged in on their fifteenth wedding anniversary.

This time, Tina their twelve-year-old daughter was with them. Tina and her parents were aware how special this treat was. After eight hours of a gruelling drive, with a couple of stops enroute to rest and snack on some of their packed eats, they approached Naggar, a small town on the left bank of the Beas, about 20 kms away from the popular hill resort of Manali.

to join in the conversation with the discomforting man. Before leaving, he dug his hand into a glass jar and grabbed a couple of mouth fresheners. He placed a rupee coin on the shelf and turned away without waiting for a response from its owner.

Shaurya returned quickly to the villa through the orchard. Walking indoors, he could hear the television on high volume along with Tina's voice. Tina was watching her favourite *Shin-Chan,* still lying in the position he had left her, murmuring and smiling, frequently tilting her face towards the window.

Mona was intently reading a tourist guide to the area she had found in the rack by her bed.

'Dinner's here,' Shaurya announced to them. 'Come, Tina, who's there at the window?'

'No one, Dad. I was just mimicking *Shin-Chan*,' Tina, a great fan of the manga cartoon series, said obediently.

'This is too much!' Shaurya remonstrated. 'You need to stop, Tina. Stop behaving like a four-year-old. Come, let's eat.'

Mona looked up from her travel brochure as if she was trying to decide whether to say something or not comment altogether. It was her way of conveying to Shaurya that she knew he had smoked once again.

All that Shaurya could do was sheepishly say, 'Sorry, I had a mouth freshener but nothing can get past your inbuilt breathalyser!'

'Forget it,' she said scornfully, unpacking the food and laying it on the table. 'But tomorrow, *you* do any baby-sitting required.'

She tapped the folder she was still holding with the tip of her forefinger. 'I just read about a fabulous castle somewhere close by and I want to check it out. *On my own!*'

Tired after the daylong journey, they ate quickly and disposed of the food packets in a container with a lid, outside their door. They showered and went to bed.

Only the gurgling of the Beas flowing nearby echoed around the desolate house.

They had barely gone to sleep, when a light tap of footsteps along the wooden corridor outside, woke up Shaurya. The footsteps, seemed to be approaching from a distance. Shaurya could clearly hear soft sounds of conversation, as if someone was speaking in whispers.

The caretaker was expected only in the morning. Shaurya clearly remembered Deenu telling him that no one except them was staying in the villa.

With each approaching step, the thumping of the footsteps was getting louder and soon he could feel the vibrations on the wooden floor.

As the whispers and tapping of steps drew closer, he could hear that the sounds were of youngsters: kids and adolescents. Certainly, these were odd hours for children to be roaming about.

Shaurya moved his quilt away, stepped out of the bed

and looked through the keyhole in the door. Through that tiny keyhole in the dark passage, he could see faint human images. Then he saw three figures floating ahead, in a cloud of smoke. Naked and barefoot. One of them was limping, gliding mid-air.

Two of them appeared to be in their early teens, while the third one seemed younger. He moved between the other two with difficulty, leaning on their shoulders. His face looked charred, features melted under a scalp of hair, still alight. The other two appeared to be made up of only ash. An unbearable stench of burning flesh that could only be human was filtering through the keyhole. The smell was very much like that of burning flesh in an open cremation ground.

The boys coughed and coughed, gesturing with scorched pleading arms towards the door as if begging Shaurya to open it. Something—*an instinct for self-preservation, and a desire to protect his family*—made him refuse.

His fingers froze on the inner lock of the door, holding it fast, while his eyes and senses remained glued to the pitiful sights and sounds beyond it. The boys grew more desperate. The youngest one was wailing in a high-pitched voice, as a remnant of his ear detached itself from his skull and fell to the ground.

'Get us some water buckets and sand please!' wailed the boys. 'We will either suffocate in this smoke or die in the flames!' Their coughing turned to retching noises.

Unable to respond to their pleas, Shaurya struggled to open his mouth that some strong force had clamped shut.

The smoke and the suffocating stench now percolated from the keyhole and the little empty space from the bottom of the door. The whispered pleadings of the dreaded visitors now became a loud noise.

He turned, very, very slowly towards Mona and Tina. They were both asleep, completely unaware of the horror outside their door. The repeated thump against the door had become insistent, almost bordering on violent. The dark brown heavy wooden door could break down anytime soon and the restless figures could smash their way into the room.

There was a jiggle—a rough, impatient wrestling with the creaking door handle. Shaurya held his breath, staring at the wooden door, afraid it could break anytime. Outside, the children wandered lost between the smoke that engulfed them. The wood around the lock creaked under the pressure, and his fear rose with the sickening noise.

Shaurya was suffocated by the smoke and stench. His eyes shut and he slumped to the floor amidst the fading noises.

***

'Papa, get up! Get *up*, Papa! You promised us we'd go jogging by the river! And then Mama can go off to do her own thing right after.'

Tina was trying to wake Shaurya up from what looked like deep sleep.

He opened his eyes and saw Mona and Tina dressed in their tracksuits and jogging shoes. His eyes swung towards the wooden door and the lock, still in position. He went to the door and gingerly unlocked it, pushing it open.

Faint wisps of smoke, *or was it ordinary mountain mist* was still in the corridor. Yet he knew he would never get the odour of the night out of his mind.

As planned, they trekked to the river. He found himself holding Tina tight as they walked, and watched with greater care as Mona and Tina took selfies by the rushing water. They hadn't eaten since the night and were soon hungry in the brisk air.

Shaurya had an idea.

'Let me get us a good, hot breakfast from the *dhaba*. Then we can drive together beyond Atal tunnel today,' he said. He trotted off in the direction of the food joint, before Mona could insist on having things her own way

The market was still closed, but *'Fauji da Dhaba'* had opened barely a few minutes earlier. Shaurya was the first and only customer at the time.

After ordering a spread of his family's favourites with sealed glasses of sweet, hot masala chai, Shaurya looked towards the banyan tree to see if the cigarette vendor had arrived.

The old man was there, setting up his vend for the day.

'*Babaji,* can you quickly fish out a fag for me?' Shaurya asked him, looking as guilty as a schoolboy sneaking a fag.

The man looked knowing as he performed the ritual of the day before, bringing the cigarette closer to his nostrils to identify the brand before handing it over to him.

'Was there a fire in this locality at night?' Shaurya asked him, taking a deep drag.

'Fire? Of course! Don't you know? You're staying there. Oh, I forgot, you're new here,' the man croaked. 'And that happened fifty years ago.'

Shaurya looked at him aghast.

'Woods Villa used to be a boy's hostel for the Riverdale Higher Secondary School. It housed fifty teenagers whose families lived too far away for the boys to come and go daily.'

'But why the fire?' Shaurya had to prod the old man into speaking.

'There was a break for Dussehra, a very important festival in this area. Most of the children had gone home for the vacation. The four that were left were forced to stay because a landslide in their villages prevented their parents from picking them up.

'It was late October then and the nights could be chilling, especially by the riverside. The boys had lit charcoal in the *angeethi* in the hostel to ward off the cold. There was no other heating arrangement in the building. The drunkard caretaker of the hostel was fast asleep in the nearby cottage and he had locked the hostel from outside.

'There was a storm in the night and the wooden floor caught fire from the flying embers from the *angeethi* inside the hostel. The boys tried to escape, but could not open the door to the outside. They piled up the furniture to ladder their way out and the tallest of them even managed to climb his way out after breaking open the roof. He shouted for help and tried pulling out his fellow hostel mates, but they couldn't make it through, weakened and choked with smoke as they were. The conflagration spread all over the building and it took three hours for the fire tender to arrive. By that time, the boys had perished.

'The incident occurred on the night of Amavasya and now it is said that every new moon, the spirits of the three boys roam around in the vicinity begging for blankets and water to save themselves.

'Last night was Amavasya.'

'But you said... you said...,' stuttered Shaurya, 'you said *three* of them. What happened to the fourth, the tallest one, who had managed to escape by breaking open the rooftop?'

'He survived, but he was severely burned and he even lost his eyesight,' said the man, with a tired sigh.

'Where is he now? Do you know him?'

Shaurya was still sceptical about the veracity of the incident.

'Of course,' the old man said bitterly.

'That blind, disfigured boy has grown into an old man who now owns and operates a small vend.'

The man's fingers trembled as he peeled off the dark glasses from his face.

Shaurya leaned in, his gaze locking into the ravaged face—wrinkled skin, beard streaked with grey and angry pink scars snaking around a mangled nose. The glasses dropped. Shaurya froze. Where eyes should have been, there were only two hollow pits—no iris, no pupil, just raw, unblinking voids that swallowed the light and amplified the silence.

RIVER MAN—THE SAVIOUR

'They say the dead don't speak, but sometimes, we shout. Especially when life is worth saving.'

For Rajneesh Dave, a twenty-eight-year-old, IAS probationer from Bhavnagar in Gujarat, the trip was becoming nostalgic.

Kullu-Manali Valley stirred something in him—fifteen years had passed since he had last been here, as a boy accompaniedd by his parents and little sister Jahanvi.

After his training in the academy at Mussoorie, he was on his first posting in Banjar, a small town on the left bank of Beas about 60 kilometres away from Kullu.

Now as his Gypsy wound along the mountain road, towards his new home, a burst of noise broke the stillness—splashing, shouts, laughter. Below a raft bobbed through the rapids, packed with grinning youngsters and instructors in fluorescent jackets. Rajneesh slowed instinctively, watching them navigate the river's wild pulse. Their playful antics took Rajneesh down memory lane. The Valley had not changed, not really.

He asked his driver to halt, while he watched them ply their oars; his thoughts went back to a summer, years ago.

He was thirteen years old then and his sister Jahanvi barely eight. Rajneesh recalled vividly—despite the now depleted cover of trees—that they had been on the same stretch where they had halted for tea and snacks. A blue board was nailed to a naked banyan tree and proclaimed in red bold letters: 'RAVE AND RAFT.' It still stood as tall as it had more than a decade-and-a-half ago, except that it had now been denuded of its rich foliage.

It was the same signboard that had grabbed Rajneesh's attention as a teenager. He had watched a group of tourists preparing to go rafting excitedly harnessing their safety gear, and he had persuaded his father to let the family join them.

Though hesitant initially, his father had finally relented reassured by the site's instructor, a robust man in his forties who promised there would be no danger. The four-km ride from Pirdi to Nagwai, he assured him, was one of the safest routes. Eight people and the instructor who introduced himself as Ruldu Ram had soon pushed the raft into the river. Rajneesh's parents joined the holiday-makers' laughter, while Jahanvi's eyes widened at the sensation of being buoyed up by the waters of the raging river.

But no one had suspected how strong the current would be that day. Rajneesh heard Ruldu Ram shout a warning when their raft hit a boulder and tilted toppling Jahanvi over the side into the froth. Rajneesh's parents and the other tourists managed to cling to the raft shouting for help. Ruldu Ram lost no time and leaped over the edge into the rapid waters. He held Jahanvi firmly with one hand while he held the hooks of the raft with the other. Soon, the raft overturned completely and spun dangerously into a whirlpool.

The ordeal continued for a while, with desperate screams for help from those trapped in the swirl and anxious shouts from the onlookers, but no rescue team was in sight.

Finally, Ruldu Ram, in what seemed a feat of magic, managed to push the raft out of the hidden undertow, all while keeping a firm grip on Jahnvi's arm. His strong legs thrashed against the flow, while he pushed himself onto the inverted raft, and pulled up the others, one by one, after him. He masterfully wielded an oar to steer them to the river bank, with their lives and limbs intact.

Everyone heaved a sigh of relief and praised their rescuer amid thunderous applause and Rajneesh too found a new hero in Ruldu Ram. But the man of the moment played down his act of bravery.

'That was just another small skirmish with the river,' he said dismissively. 'They keep happening.'

***

'Sirji, it's getting late.' The voice of Rajneesh's driver brought him back to the present. The rafting party had left and there was no one else around. So, Rajneesh resumed his journey home.

Home was a 'dak bungalow'—as such remote government guest houses were called in the day—close to Banjar town. No more than seventy small households made up the community. Rajneesh's driver carried his luggage inside and returned to his own home nearby for the night promising to be back at 8 am the next morning. There was a part-time caretaker-cum-cook at the bungalow, Nikka Ram, who lived in his quarters nearby.

After having eaten a well-cooked dinner, an exhausted Rajneesh retired straightway to his room. He was to meet some local officials early the next day. Nikka Ram thoughtfully placed a jug of water and a tumbler on Rajneesh's bedside table. Before turning to leave, he asked an unexpected question of his new sahib.

'Sahibji, do you believe in ghosts?'

Rajneesh, a postgraduate in mathematics and a hard-boiled rationalist, shot him a look of derision. 'Certainly not, Nikka Ram. Do you?' Nikka left the room with a disbelieving smirk.

It was 11 at night before Rajneesh finished reviewing his schedule for the next day. Since a bulb illuminated the area outside the bungalow, he decided to switch off the ones in his own room and turned in wearily for the night.

By the time the flickering bulb outside went off completely, Rajneesh was in deep sleep, oblivious to the rustling leaves and the breeze that had begun rattling the windows. Nikka had not closed the windows firmly enough and the rising wind sent the panes rattling and the curtains fluttering. The combined noise disturbed Rajneesh. He got up and tried to secure the windows more firmly, though this was hard against the strong wind.

He had barely drifted back to sleep when he heard a loud thud. Something heavy had fallen on him. Already curled up in a quilt, he found it difficult to push the heavy thing aside. Somehow, he managed to free his head and what he saw caused him to open his mouth in a terrified scream, except that it couldn't escape his throat.

A skeleton had fallen over him—out of nowhere it seemed. It was chalk-white and featureless and yet, there was a frightening red glimmer emanating from the empty holes where its eyes had once been.

Soon the skinless and brittle bones of his hands descended on Rajneesh. They clamped themselves coldly around Rajneesh's throat and though he tried as hard as he could, he couldn't shake off their deathly grasp.

Rajneesh gasped, trying to suck in air, but his airway seemed to have been blocked. A rattling noise escaped his throat, a desperate plea for some oxygen. Deathly fear paralysed him for a fleeting moment, as his senses grew numb.

'This can't be real—it must be a nightmare,' he thought. But the cold, bony grip tightening around his windpipe felt terrifyingly suffocating and real.

He thrashed wildly, his arms flailing in a bid to dislodge the skeleton, but to no avail. The weight on his chest was crushing and taking away his breath. Rajneesh could only think of those bony fingers digging deep into his throat.

As the hollow sockets of the skull came closer to his face, he could hear the rasping sound of his own strangled breaths. The cold and empty voice of death now pressed down on him.

Unable to fight it off or even to cry for help, just when he was about to surrender, a loud noise shattered the silence; the windowpane burst as a piece of rock thrown by an unseen force flew into the room and landed on the floor.

He woke up.

He gulped down his glass of water and looked around him. There seemed to be no clue to the night's happenings, save for the gaping hole in the glass window and the large stone on the floor. Yet to recover from the suffocation, his vision still blurred, Rajneesh noticed black spots dancing at the edges of his eyes.

He could see nothing outside. Unable to sleep a wink, he left the room for some fresh air and time to think.

Close to the entrance of the guesthouse, he saw the shadow of a figure under the streetlight. Rajneesh raced towards it and was relieved to find it was a human being. The stranger in the night had a greying beard, but the athletic physique of a younger man. A black blanket partly covered his torso revealing a fluorescent vest beneath. He held a torch, which he was directing at the window of Rajneesh's room, where those white curtains were still billowing in the cold night wind.

Rajneesh, relieved to see a real human being, pounced on the man.

'Are you the *chowkidaar* here?' he demanded. 'Did you notice anyone entering the guesthouse?'

The man, however, seemed unmoved. 'You must be dreaming, Sirji,' the man chuckled, still directing the torch light on the window.

Rajneesh let go of his embarrassment at being laughed at by a stranger and admitted that he might have indeed had a bad dream.

'They scare you almost to death,' the man said, as if familiar with the situation.

'What, the dreams?' Rajneesh asked him, more confused than ever.

'No, *sirji,* the ghosts in this dak bungalow,' he said calmly. 'I was outside the garden when I heard a scream from your room. I didn't know someone was staying there as such noises during the night are common here,' he went on.

A longer explanation followed. 'This bungalow is

more than a hundred years old,' the man said.

'Beside it, once stood a temporary jail, used during the British regime to confine hardened criminals. The room where you slept, it's said, was the very place, where the ones sentenced to death were hanged.

'You were lucky to have woken up in time. A few years ago, a young woman tourist was found dead in the same room. She had gone to sleep and simply did not wake up in the morning.'

Rajneesh, ever the cynic, didn't want to be convinced easily. 'Are you sure these are not just stories cooked up to thrill tourists and increase the mysterious attraction of the place?' he asked the man teasingly. 'How long have you been here, anyway? And what do you do?'

The man answered gravely, 'I have been a member of a rescue and instructors' team for adventure sports in the area. We run an adventure activities club near Pirdi. I lost my left limb, while rescuing a group of tourists when a raft overturned. So, I can no longer accompany people during the run or in the river. But I try to help in demonstrating rescue tactics. It's just a part-time job during the day. But at night I double up as a watchman. It's not a strain even for a cripple like me, since I hardly sleep anyway.'

Rajneesh's memory of his childhood adventure came flooding back. 'Are you Ruldu Ram? You once saved our lives when our raft capsized many years ago,' he asked hesitantly, his tone full of respect.

'Yes, *Sirji*,' the man smiled with his old, now familiar humility. 'Such incidents are part of our lives. They keep happening. No need to glorify them.'

He limped away leaning on a strong knobbed cane, but not before telling Rajneesh that he should keep the lights of his room on and call for help if he noticed anything unusual.

Sleep came reluctantly to Rajneesh for the remainder of that night. He woke up the next morning only when he heard the doorbell ring announcing the return of the caretaker, Nikka Ram to the dak bungalow.

He skipped breakfast and crisply concluded his introductions to the local officials, since Rajneesh wanted to get to the district headquarters in Kullu in good time. He squeezed a tip into Nikka Ram's pocket, returned his sheepish salute, and climbed into the front of his Gypsy next to the driver.

But once they had crossed the bridge and come again to the familiar stretch—the old blue board against the leafless trunk of the banyan tree; the river swirling below them and early-bird youngsters already flocking to board their rafts in a flutter of fluorescent bodysuits—he couldn't resist a brief stop hoping to meet Ruldu Ram there again.

'Let's have a quick cup of tea and snacks here,' he told the driver.

Rajneesh sipped his tea, waiting for one of the training sessions to be over and still looking for Ruldu Ram. Soon the group dispersed and the tourists were seen harnessing their safety gear, preparing to enter the water.

Rajneesh approached the eldest of the instructors. 'Excuse me. I need to meet a person called Ruldu Ramji. Do you know where I can find him?'

The instructor seemed surprised at the question.

'He is no longer with us. He's dead,' he said briefly, before returning his watchful gaze to the river revellers.

'But I met him only last night!' Rajneesh blurted, feeling foolish all over again.

The instructor, however, seemed hardly surprised.

'Sure,' he said, nodding casually. 'People keep coming across him often, particularly those who are in trouble.'

Realising Rajneesh had no clue about what had transpired over the years, the instructor began to explain.

'As a matter of fact, we started holding these demonstrations and mock rescue operations here only after his death, some ten years ago.

'It all started from the time we were accompanying some college students on an expedition, failing to notice that the raft was overloaded. While we were travelling towards Bhuntar where the flow is rapid, we found ourselves stuck between jagged boulders and tilting dangerously.

'Ruldu Ram, as he always did in such situations, quickly jumped into the river, and started pulling the raft away from the boulders, even ducking underwater to push it upwards. He succeeded all right—he always had before—but this time, he found his leg trapped between two closely packed rocks. So rapid was the flow of water that other rescuers could not get near enough to him to extricate him from that tragic trap. By the time the backup team was rushed in from Kullu, Ruldu Ram had stopped breathing.'

Rajneesh asked dumbly, 'Was it only his spirit, then, that I spoke to last night?'

'Hmm… where was this?' mused the instructor. 'Was it outside the dak bungalow near Banjar?'

He seemed to know the answer and continued: 'That bungalow has a dark past. Locals believed, till a decade ago, that whoever spent a night in it, died there in his sleep. The last victim was an Italian tourist although it was said to be a case of a heart attack. Ruldu Ram was born and raised in that area and would tell us that the bungalow had always been haunted. As children, they had been taught to fear it and had been told that it would bring instant death to anyone who entered it. This had left a lasting impression on his boyhood and he had never ever dared to cross its threshold even as an adult.

'A day before he drowned trying to save people, he told us out of the blue that he would continue to save lives even after his death—whether in his natural habitat, the water, or on the land of his birthplace. And ever since Ruldu Ram died, not a single death has been reported there, although some occasional visitors have reported some weird happenings at night when they are sleeping.'

And so it is that tales of Ruldu Ram, the rescuer and a legend born from the Beas's current and from the hearts of those he saved, just keep going on—a timeless sentinel against the watery depths and mountainous heights of the region.

THE CALLER DOES NOT EXIST!

'They say the house still echoes with the cries of children. Every floorboard remembers the weight of small feet that will never run again. When you build on bones, don't be surprised when the house bleeds.'

It was Mahesh's second week at the newly set up fast food kitchen at Scandal Point in Shimla. He was wiping the counter, while scanning the day's menu on the tent card, next to him. A bigger menu beside it, also displayed the mobile number and the app that could be downloaded to order those items that were on special offer.

A dedicated mobile phone was also placed on the counter to attend to calls requesting home delivery. The insta-kitchen wore its unusual name on its tiny shop front:

'DIALLED & DELIVERED.'

Its unstated USP was clear: Speed and efficiency.

Although a recent fixture in town, the joint had quickly created a buzz for its range of rich but affordable old-fashioned soup-and-sandwich combos, each like a full meal for someone who was really hungry.

Mahesh, a native of Dehradun in Uttarakhand, had

come to Shimla some two years earlier. After a succession of small jobs in *dhabas* and then as a delivery boy with a local *kirana* shop, he found employment at *Dialled & Delivered,* through the recommendation of one of his loyal customers, a retired army officer to whose house Mahesh used to regularly deliver commodities on his bicycle.

'Colonel *Saab*,' as Mahesh called him, took a liking to the fresh-faced, smiling boy who supplied him milk and eggs daily even at the height of winter, wheeling through banks of snow with an uncomplaining willingness that the old soldier respected.

A former colleague of Colonel *Saab* owned the new fast-food joint. He too was pleased to have found Mahesh, who had already become an asset to the joint that promised to deliver any order within a radius of 10 km within half an hour.

Besides being quick on his feet, Mahesh was a skilled scooter driver who could zip through short cuts with speed and precision, even at a moment's notice. He was a perfect choice for a hot-food delivery boy.

Besides Mahesh and a co-worker, Bunty, the place had a fast-food cook and a cashier, who doubled as the manager. With an increasing customer base, additional staff was to be hired soon. Meanwhile, the onus fell on Mahesh to ensure that orders were delivered on time and the service continued to get a good rating from clients.

Despite the exhaustion the job brought on, Mahesh

was happy as it not only offered him almost double his previous salary, but also a fancy scooter that prominently displayed the name of his food outlet along with its mobile number.

As Mahesh readied the joint that day, the mobile on the counter rang and a number flashed on the screen.

'Good afternoon!' he said politely into the piece. '"Dialled & Delivered". What would you like to order?'

'One large French Onion Soup and six Cheese Sandwiches please. And a small salad on the side,' a child said eagerly. 'And please make it fast!' The voice appeared to be that of a young girl.

'Sure, Ma'am! Your address please?'

'It's the Campbell House—everyone knows it—below Navbahar Road,' said the girl, speaking rapidly, in short, pleading sentences. 'Near the cemetery. Please make it quick. We are so very hungry! We'll pay cash on delivery.' The voice crackled and the call was disconnected.

He quickly shared the details with the rapid-order cook and began to look for his gloves and helmet. He had to ensure that the delivery was made well on time—or pay for the special himself.

The order was ready within 10 minutes.

'Take care of the counter and don't take orders till I come back. I'll be back soon,' Mahesh said to Bunty as he quickly grabbed the packet containing two sealed plastic bowls of soup and salad, and a package of sandwiches neatly wrapped in wax paper. He sprinted to his two-wheeler, which he had parked below Mall Road, near the lift and dashed towards Navbahar.

There was a traffic snarl on the way. It was the tourist season, but Mahesh had confidence in his navigating skills. He outrode the passing four-wheelers in minutes. He had fed the Campbell House address into the GPS of his mobile and was soon just 2 km from his destination. The map showed a diversion towards a narrow *kutcha* path surrounded by white and yellow flowers and dotted with Deodars. This was a rare untouched area in Shimla that had turned so much greenery into concrete. Only a few houses were around, some with big and slanting rooftops, typical of the British era.

Mahesh slowed down on the bumpy path and began to move past their gates. No numbers were displayed at the entrances. Still, he followed the Google map voice, which soon declared, 'Your destination is on the right.'

A big, rusty iron gate at the entrance greeted him. He stopped and took the sturdy package out of the locked boot of his scooter. He had to force open the gate with its creaky hinges that revealed a double-storey building. A bell at the door carried a gilt nameplate with the owner's name in italics: *Campbell.*

Mahesh pressed the bell and waited for the door to open. No one turned up for a while.

He pressed it a couple of times more and heard its

ring echoing inside the house. When no one answered, he pushed the door that opened with a grating sound. He found himself inside a large hall, its wooden floorboards in disrepair. The hall was partitioned by a translucent curtain that offered only a glimpse of what lay beyond.

Some of the furniture, including what looked like a sofa set and a table, was draped with a dusty white sheet. Wooden stairs led up to the first floor. The room appeared uninhabited for years save for the glowing chandelier that hung from the high ceiling in the centre. A golden telephone on an antique wooden stool, caught his eye, its cradle engraved with unique carvings.

He waited.

Footsteps echoed down the staircase. They belonged to a middle-aged woman in a shabby housecoat. Her hair was a tangled mess of strands, and hid her pale face. She advanced slowly, gazed at the telephone expressionlessly and then turned towards the curtain that divided the hall.

Suddenly her expression shifted. Anger flickered on her pale face. She turned back to him her gaze sharp and questioning.

'Ma'am, I'm here with your order for our soup-and-sandwich special.'

She turned to the area that had been curtained-off and with her authoritative fingers, summoned some smaller blurred figures in the shadows, behind the overhanging material. They were children–one was a white-skinned girl whom he thought might have made the call. She gestured quietly for him to place the packet on a small dust-covered table. The other was probably her younger brother.

Unusually silent and shy, they were staring at the package with strange expressions of mixed fear and longing on their faces. The cold hall smelt of damp and mildew, but the warmth emanating from the carry-bag seemed to have brought on a voracious appetite.

Mahesh felt uncomfortable and felt the need to exit the house quickly.

'Please enjoy your soup, while it's hot and kindly give us a good rating in the feedback,' he said, smiling professionally at the children and the woman.

By way of answer, the woman clicked her fingers for the children to go inside.

Mahesh wondered if she'd forgotten she needed to pay. 'Ma'am, you'd opted for cash on delivery,' he prompted her.

'Comes to Rs 350, with Rs 50 extra for the salad,' he informed her, holding out the bill.

She made no move to take it, but strode forward to the curtain and pushed it aside.

He watched as she opened the packet of sandwiches, balled one of them tightly in her fist and smeared the leaking mayonnaise over the little girl's face. Then, she yanked the girl closer to her and pushed the sandwich into her resisting mouth.

Mahesh stood transfixed as the girl gasped for breath

and desperately tried to push away the older woman's sinewy hand from her face. The little boy, unaware of the proceedings, drummed his legs on the sides of the chair on which he was seated. The girl, unable to free herself, collapsed to the side. The woman now turned to the boy.

Mahesh desperately wanted to go to the children's aid, but was unable to move. All he could see now was the woman's back and her tattered gown. The boy was now making the same choking noises, his legs now kicking frantically as the woman appeared to upend the bowl of soup over him.

Shaken from his stupor, Mahesh looked around and spotted a paperweight on the small table, which still held some of the food the children had desperately craved for. He picked up the heavy stone object and threw it at the woman. To his disbelief, the round and heavy paperweight passed through her white gown without hitting her and stopped at the window behind. The woman, who still clasped the boy, seemed unruffled by the goings-on, and was not even slightly distracted.

Suddenly, the aroma of chicken and black pepper, which had pervaded the room vanished and all that Mahesh could sense was the nauseating smell of decaying flesh.

He reached numbly into his pocket for his mobile, but realised he had forgotten to remove it from the holder on the handle of his scooter.

Unable to think of what to do next, he dashed to the

side table, lifted the receiver of the rotary phone, and began to dial the police control room.

The perforated graphite circle seemed to take so long to dial 100!

It was only later that a startled Mahesh realised that there was no dial tone. As he looked at the phone more carefully, he found it had no connecting cord.

The woman now turned towards Mahesh and was staring at him from behind her dishevelled hair.

A horrified Mahesh did not know what to do.

Things around him were turning upside down.

With his heart pounding in terror, he turned abruptly and fled towards the gate, his footsteps echoing ominously on the cold, silent wooden floor behind him.

Somehow, he found himself outside the hall. The big entrance oak door slammed shut behind him on its own. Leaping onto his scooter, he drove at a speed he'd never attempted before.

The winding road seemed to twist and turn unnaturally, shrouded in an eerie mist that obscured familiar landmarks. Each moment felt like eternity. The air seemed thick with a palpable sense of dread as Mahesh raced his scooter towards 'Dialled & Delivered.'

His mind replayed the haunting events at the hall—the mysterious woman, flickering shadows and the muffled voices of the children that echoed through empty corridors as he stumbled off his scooter near the Mall

Road, breathless and trembling.

Time seemed to warp and stretch, distorting reality as he arrived at Dialled & Delivered in what felt like an eternity. His eyes darted nervously as he looked back again and again, wondering if he had truly escaped the malevolent presence that lurked in the ancient building.

At the counter, his partner was counting the cash before leaving for the day.

'What took you so long, Mahesh?' Bunty asked him peevishly. 'You spent the whole day on just one order!'

Then, seeing Mahesh's ashen face, he asked with concern, 'What happened?'

'I made a delivery to the Campbell House in Navbahar,' Mahesh said, panting. 'I-t, i-t, it was a difficult ride.'

'Where in Navbahar ? Not the cemetery road, surely?' persisted Bunty with a look of disbelief.

Mahesh read out the address on the small notepad where he had jotted it down before leaving to deliver the order.

'What? Why didn't you tell me before leaving that you were going there instead of just writing it down?'

Mahesh was still breathing heavily when Bunty finished his story.

'The house belonged to Brigadier Campbell, you idiot,' he'd begun in a scolding tone. 'Don't tell me that you hadn't been told about him in the two years you've spent in Shimla?'

Mahesh dumbly shook his head.

'Brigadier Campbell,' Bunty continued, 'was a widower who'd served in the British Army here. He stayed back after Independence. He fell in love with Rosie Jones, the cook at a local patisserie, who made the most delicious bread and savouries in town, partly because he enjoyed her kind of western food so far from his own home in England.

'Rosie obliged his taste in both women and cuisine by marrying him. Her liking for Brigadier Campbell, however, did not extend to his children. And when, a few months later, the man died in a road accident and his lawyer told Rosie that he had named his two children as the only heirs in his will, she was far from pleased. That she was named their guardian till the time they grew up, was not enough for the greedy woman.'

'W-what do you mean?' said Mahesh. But in his heart, he already knew.

'Well,' said Bunty, 'it is believed that after several months of neglecting them to the point of starvation, she poisoned the two children and buried them in the backyard of the house.

'To all the neighbours who asked where the children were, she said that she sent them to a boarding school as she was finding it difficult to look after them. But neighbours had already known of her cruelty to her late husband's girl and boy, even as her own bakery continued to thrive as she catered to the needs of customers in the locality in which she lived.

'A few years later, somewhere in the mid-'70s, there was a massive landslide at midnight and the entire house collapsed on itself. Rosie Jones was believed to have died in the tragedy.

This baffled Mahesh and he couldn't help interjecting, 'But the house is intact! I've seen it with my own eyes, inside out. It even had a nameplate!'

Bunty looked at him and resumed, 'Just wait, I'm not finished yet. A distant relative of Brigadier Campbell's decided to rebuild the house so that he could convert it into a homestay. It was during the construction that the corpses of the children were discovered among the ruins.

'The homestay only ran for a few weeks. Guests who stayed there reported hearing disturbing cries of invisible children at night begging to be fed, only to be abruptly muffled. The guests also complained of the obnoxious smell of rotten flesh that wafted in through their windows. Locals believe that the ghosts of the hungry children and of Rosie still haunt the house.

'The homestay was closed as people were scared by the stories told by previous guests. But it is said that many eateries with home delivery services in the town continued to receive orders for sundry European items from children over the phone, who would cite Campbell House as their address. Initially, some delivery boys went there and were baffled by their experiences, which they were too afraid to describe.

'As word spread in the town, few dared to entertain the calls from Campbell House. Rumours started doing the rounds that the orders were fake, mere pranks orchestrated by mischievous youngsters. And soon, no one answered those calls.'

Still sceptical of what Bunty had recounted, Mahesh took the mobile phone from its place on the shop counter and scrolled through the call log, scrutinising the list thoroughly.

His search stopped at a call that was made from a landline before he last left the shop:

0177-22##99

Mahesh quickly dialled the number, using his true caller service to find out the identity of the caller. While he waited for the call to get through, he noticed the true caller flashing 'Campbell'.

The call did not happen, eventually.

An electronic recorded voice informed Mahesh, 'The number you have dialled does not exist.'

MYSTERIOUS PILLION RIDER

'Some passengers just leave a chill you can't shake off.'

Rocky was in a heightened state of excitement. He had just bought a spanking new Royal Enfield Hunter 350 with the savings from his very first job—money that he had carefully squirrelled away over the course of an entire year.

Still a research scholar pursuing his doctorate, Rocky had joined a private university near Shoghi, about twenty kilometres from Shimla as a lecturer. Teaching was his passion, but what thrilled him just as much was the daily ride of over fifty kilometres from his home in Mashobra to the university campus and back. On his precious new possession, the *vroom* at the touch of the accelerator echoed around the mountains as he swung left and right down the serpentine road. It made him feel like a real *man*—a *macho* man!

It was a cold January night, and Rocky was riding home once again on the wheels of his strong metal companion, after attending a farewell party for a colleague.

His obsession with the new bike had become a running joke among his friends, who teased him that he no longer needed a life partner now. Even during that evening's revelry, one of them had ribbed him: 'Will we ever see someone riding pillion behind you or will you keep biking around the hills alone?'

'Will bring her along next time for sure,' Rocky had responded sportingly, downing his sixth shot of tequila before bidding a noisy farewell to his departing friend and leaping onto the still as-good-as-new Royal Enfield.

It had begun to snow, and Rocky was keen to reach home before the road iced over. Negotiating sharp turns on hilly terrain would be tricky. Within half an hour, every surface around him had turned white.

As he approached the petrol pump just before the famous St Bede's College of Navbahar, he noticed someone waving at him from the side of the road. His headlight illuminated a woman in a full-length formal dress; her thumb raised up in the universal language of hitchhikers.

No other vehicle was visible on that stretch, nor was there any sign of habitation. Only an old disused water source marked the spot. Rocky was aware that isolated, poorly-lit stretches around the township had recently gained notoriety for the shady activities of drug-abusers and call girls. But it appeared too late at night for even those individuals to be operating and the woman certainly looked as though she might be in trouble.

She was a fair-skinned woman and quite young. Her hair was loose and unusually long, almost brushing the ground. She wore long gloves that reached up her arms, like the ones that Rocky had seen in ballroom scenes from period movies.

'Do you need any help? Can I drop you off somewhere?' he asked politely.

She didn't reply but smiled faintly in the dim light and stepped towards the rear of his bike.

A sozzled Rocky conjured up a vision of a beautiful damsel sitting behind him, leaning on his shoulders, her arms encircling his waist from behind and whispering sweet nothings into his ear, her perfumed face close to his. Oh! To impress his friends with this miracle!

Though he had always brushed off their teasing about the lack of a girlfriend, the jibes had stung. Ever since buying his new bike, he had secretly longed for a beautiful pillion rider who would be the envy of everyone he knew.

But Rocky had a weakness—he was painfully shy when it came to breaking the ice with strangers, especially young women.

Amid these thoughts, he felt a tap on his shoulder. It was a clear signal for him to ride on. He wasted no time in pressing the accelerator, setting his two-wheeler in motion. The roar of the machine down that empty road left no scope for any conversation.

Rocky grew restless. He had finally got a pretty woman

onto his bike, and here he was struggling even to ask her name or where she wanted to go.

After a few minutes, they reached the bus stop at Sanjauli, a small township about eight kilometres from his home. Rocky could no longer delay his questions.

'Where exactly do I drop you off?' he finally asked, half preparing himself for a supplementary query about her home address and if all went well, her phone number.

But the woman remained silent.

Assuming she hadn't heard him over the noise his bike made, Rocky repeated the question, this time more loudly.

'Ma'am! Where can I drop you off?'

Still, complete silence.

Puzzled, Rocky slowed down and stopped his two-wheeler under a streetlight.

'Ma'am?'

Raising the visor of his helmet, he turned to look back at the pillion rider.

The seat was empty.

Befuddled, Rocky resumed his journey home, alone, with only the fog for company.

Those spooky tales his college mates had shared—stories of mysterious women appearing along that very stretch—suddenly seemed less like fiction.

Ghost stories abounded in Shimla as in any other hill station. They had once been favourite bedtime tales for Rocky and his friends. None of them had ever encountered a ghost in real life, but no one had doubted the truth of those narrations either.

For twenty-five-year-old Rocky, this was a first—if it could be called an encounter. He realised he was sweating despite the freezing weather. He sped home.

Later, when he recounted the incident to his friends, they laughed it off as wishful thinking.

'This is what happens when you keep longing for a partner for a joy ride and do nothing about it. Then you turn your fantasy into reality under the influence of tequila,' his ex-colleague, Rajesh, teased with a wink.

'Time to find a partner and get married!' his friend's wife added.

Rocky was almost convinced that he'd imagined the whole thing.

Days passed.

Yet whenever he rode through that stretch in the evenings or at night, the memory of the mysterious woman who had vanished from his bike would send a chill down his spine.

Still, he would glance around, hoping, just faintly that he might see her again, with her flowing hair and silent smile.

Weeks went by and the town began to look forward to the end of winter. The wedding date of another colleague arrived and a gala event was scheduled at a famous hotel in Chaura Maidan. To add to the festivities, it coincided with Valentine's Day.

The party stretched past midnight. This time it was the drizzle outside that prompted Rocky to leave before the rain worsened. He congratulated the newlyweds and promised to catch up after their honeymoon, then headed off. He had forgotten his raincoat and was spattered by the rain, but was grateful there was no fog. He could see the road ahead clearly.

As he passed through Chotta Shimla and approached the familiar petrol station, he thought he saw a human figure standing at the same spot as before. His bike screeched to a halt almost before he realised it.

He knew the meaning of the feeling now: déjà vu.

The long-haired young woman in a gown was smiling at him again, gesturing for a lift. Rocky felt a mix of fear and curiosity.

'Where the hell did you disappear last time? Are you for real or did I imagine you?' he asked, surprising himself. He no longer struggled to start a conversation.

The woman kept smiling, her gaze locked into Rocky's eyes.

'You're a man in a hurry. You didn't even let me sit down on your bike last time. Before I could sit, you sped off and left me behind,' she pouted, stroking her long hair with hands now bare—without gloves, just pale hands with unvarnished nails.

Rocky stared at her in disbelief. He had been absent-minded on many occasions and was quite capable of such goof-ups. His mother had often scolded him for forgetting the vegetables at the vendors or milk packets at the booth after paying for them.

Perhaps all that tequila had caused him to forget to wait for her to be seated the last time. Guilt washed over him.

'I am so sorry, Beautiful Lady,' he said in a formal voice full of regret.

'Apologies for my conduct. I was drunk and—you're right—I was probably in a tearing hurry.'

Her smile turned sardonic. 'You don't look sober today either,' she tittered.

Rocky gestured for her to climb on and kept the bike steady until he was sure she was seated comfortably on the elevated pillion.

He felt the familiar tap on his shoulder and reassured, he took off. He could feel her arms around his waist as he shifted gears and tilted his bike around hairpin bends.

'You really scared the hell out of me last time,' he said. 'It's good that we met again today or I'd never known if the last time really happened.'

The beautiful lady gave no reply, but Rocky could feel her presence through the familiar fragrance of jasmine that lingered around her.

Sanjauli township and the bus stop were still more than a kilometre away, and they had just reached Navbahar Bus Stop outside St Bede's college.

How do I ask her when I can see her again? Would it be too rude to ask for her phone number? Rocky was caught in a dilemma, and was lost in thought when suddenly his bike hit a speed breaker and wobbled dangerously. He felt the pillion-rider's hands clutch wildly at his back and chest, the grip sharp and painful, as she tried to regain her balance. Somehow, he managed to steady the bike and rode on murmuring an apology.

'I'm so sorry,' he said, deeply embarrassed. 'It's these damned bumps on the road.'

After a while, they reached Sanjauli bus stop.

'Is this where you wanted to get off?' Rocky asked, his voice a bit uncertain as he tried to recall if she had ever mentioned her destination.

Again, no answer.

He slowed down and brought his bike to a halt under the streetlight.

'Hello! Do I drop you here?'

There was a long pause.

Rocky turned back, raising the visor of his helmet just as he had done before.

And just as before, the seat behind him was empty.

"Shithead!" he cursed himself. *"Why do I have to drink so much that I am not able to figure out what's happening for real?"*

He turned away, rode home at a furious speed, flung himself into bed and passed out.

Sunlight and the chirping of birds woke him the next morning. He was already late for university. Dashing to the bathroom, he quickly brushed and shaved. As he removed his clothes for a quick bath, something in the mirror caught his eye.

There were deep scars across his back—marks left by nails that had clawed into his skin. Blue and red bruises bloomed across his shoulders.

He remembered the tight grip of the pillion rider when he had hit the speed breaker, almost losing balance.

The memory chilled him.

HUSSY IN THE WELL

'They say she walks the corridors not to scare, but to be seen. For how long can the dead rest when their stories remain untold?'

At last, they found a place to call their own. Jimmy, Sonu and Bablu, childhood friends who had come to Dharamshala to study for their Bachelor of Business Administration, had stayed in a PG accommodation during the first week of their arrival. When both the food and accommodation proved intolerable, they rented a flat in Sidhbari, a few kilometres from the town.

The property was a double-storey house. On the first floor lived their landlord Riyaz Khan with his old and ailing mother. A construction contractor by profession, Khan travelled most of the time. He had hired a nurse to tend to the old lady twice a day. But for any emergency that arose in the middle of the night, he believed the youngsters' presence in the house would be beneficial. This expectation had been made clear to them when he rented out the ground floor of the otherwise isolated house.

When he took the advance payment, the landlord had

clearly told them that they would need to cook and clean for themselves. No maid would be allowed in. He asked for a security deposit of two months' rent and an agreement that the monthly rent thereafter would be paid before the fifth of every month. He even explained that the previous tenants, who had also been students, had left the house without paying for the month they'd stayed there—hence the necessary precaution. What he did not reveal to them was that they had left the house in a hurry!

Jimmy, Sonu, and Bablu had studied together at a day-school in Manali and this was their first experience of living away from their families. Their newly acquired flat had a small kitchen, two bedrooms and an attached bathroom. The furniture was quite basic—an antique wooden double bed, a creaking cupboard, besides a couple of new mattresses, a small stove, cooking gas, and a few utensils in the kitchen.

On their first day, they were able to clean only one of the two dank and dingy bedrooms, the one nearest the entrance. Exhausted and unaccustomed to labour, they decided to clean the other, larger bedroom, the following Sunday. All three decided to spend that night in the first room, two on the double bed and one on bedding spread on the floor.

Only Jimmy was uncomfortable sharing a room with the others. He missed the warmth of his attic at home, the cozy bed he slept in and the window next to it with a picturesque view of the green valley and the Beas River.

Sonu and Bablu were cousins, and had stayed away from home before on holidays visiting their uncle, a bachelor who was a chef in a five-star hotel in Chandigarh. Both managed to sleep easily in their new surroundings, but when Sonu started to snore, Jimmy found the noise unbearable.

He decided to move his bedding to the bigger bedroom. It was larger and had a window that looked out onto the yard outside and the fields beyond. He quickly cleaned a small portion near the cupboard, large enough to place his mattress, and lay down hoping for some restful sleep.

The entire room was dingy and damp. The window had a grill and the panoramic view of the backyard and the green fields far behind was a relief for the eyes.

Jimmy tried to sleep. They had to leave at 7.30 am the next morning to attend the orientation programme for their academic session. But even in this room, he could hear Sonu's incessant snoring.

Jimmy tossed and turned on the hard mattress, cursing his childhood friend and finally gave up in despair. He stood up and moved towards the window for some fresh air.

He saw a small lawn outside that also had a well nearby. A metal bucket attached to a pulley and a rope was gleaming in the moonlight.

Suddenly, his view was blocked by a someone who had popped out of nowhere at the window. She was an old woman. Her eyes gleamed even in the dark and her long silvery hair flowed past her shoulders almost to the ground. Her gaze was chilling and the wrinkles on her face were as deep as scars. She pressed her face into the window grill, as if trying to enter into the room. But only her long pointed nose with a glowing nose pin got past it.

'Why did you come here? You too will meet the same fate as that brazen husband-stealing hussy,' she warned in a strange growling voice.

Jimmy's throat dried up. He stood frozen, staring at the woman, trying to break open the window, pulling at the rusted iron rods with her bare hands and sharp, curved nails. Her arms and hands stretched towards him through the narrow gaps in the grill. Jimmy wanted to cry out for help, but his vocal cords seemed to be paralysed.

'Please… spare me. Go away,' he pleaded.

But the woman's menacing hands grabbed him by his hair, pulling him towards the window. Soon only the cracked grill was between him and the woman as he clung desperately to it, feeling her nails hooking onto his skull. Pain and fear gripped him, even his very breath seemed to abandon him. She seemed to be winning this grisly tug-of-war, as she pulled him out and dragged him to the corner of the lawn on which the well had been dug.

Then, still growling, she lifted him up into the air and flung him. He splashed noisily, the cold water hitting him as if it were a rock.

The next moment, he saw Sonu and Bablu standing before him, the latter with an empty bucket dangling from his hand. Jimmy found himself completely drenched in water that had spilled all over the floor of the room. And he was still holding fast onto the inner side of the window grill. Sonu and Bablu were looking at him, aghast.

'Where is she?' he asked in a trembling whisper, looking frantically around him, still feeling the bony grasp of the old woman's fingers in his hair.

'There's no one around,' Bablu told him. 'Sonu heard you murmuring in your sleep. When he came into the room, he saw you looking as if you were desperately trying to break the bars of the grill. He tried waking you up to drag you back into bed, but you resisted violently and even bit him on his hand.'

Sonu showed him the teeth marks on his wrist.

Jimmy did not know what to say. He narrated the whole incident to them.

'Stop watching all those horror shows on YouTube yaar,' Bablu said dismissively, 'Or you'll end up in the well. Come, let's finally get some sleep—but in the other room!'

Jimmy followed his friends, still too scared to look outside the window.

His mattress was completely drenched and he would have to spend the night sharing the bed with Sonu anyway.

Sonu resumed his snoring with vigour, but Jimmy was no longer complaining. The snores were comforting to hear and helped him shut off the echoes of the old woman's murderous growls.

***

Their orientation programme went off smoothly. To celebrate their induction, the three decided to go for a movie in a nearby cinema hall. They had a satisfying dinner at an eatery outside and returned to their flat shortly after ten. They slept in the same room, chatting till the wee hours and drifted off to sleep at dawn.

The next day was Sunday, and the boys busied themselves with house cleaning chores as planned. Cobwebs clung to every corner of the flat and mould had spread to the walls. Even the wooden almirah had not been spared. Some of the cobwebs were so high up the walls that Sonu could not reach them despite standing atop a table.

'I saw a long broom on the terrace when I went up to fix the dish antenna,' said Jimmy as he ran towards the stairs. 'Let me go and fetch it.'

The way to the rooftop was from the hall of the second floor. He went upstairs and knocked at the door before entering the hall. As he entered, he saw a wooden couch by the window and a dirty quilt curled over it.

He crossed the hall, ascended the stairs, and retrieved the broom from the terrace. On his way back, he was surprised to see that the couch he had passed earlier was occupied by the old woman, from the previous night. She stared at him just like before: the same piercing eyes, the wrinkled face, grey hair floating around her shoulders and pointed long nose adorned with that gleaming nose pin.

This was the woman who had tried to kill him.

Jimmy sprinted towards the door and down the stairs gasping for breath.

Sonu and Bablu refused to believe him.

'She's been bedridden for so many years and can't do a thing without the help of the nurse, for God's sake,' scoffed Bablu. 'You think she'd come downstairs looking for you, drag you from your mattress with her bare hands and make off with you from outside the grilled window?' Bablu's scornful laugh said it all.

They finally finished cleaning late in the evening. With hardly any groceries in the house, Bablu quickly prepared a simple *pulao* for dinner. Sonu, they decided would sleep alone in the second room that night and hopefully keep his snoring to himself. Sonu himself had no qualms and was happy to prove to Jimmy that his fears about the earlier night's haunting experience were baseless.

They had only been asleep for about an hour, when Jimmy was woken by the sounds from Sonu's room. He rushed, but could see nothing at first in the dark. Gradually, his eyes picked out a figure by the window.

The figure stood there clutching at the grill grimly, its entire body shivering with the effort.

shocked faces and quickly summed up the story. 'I don't know how far these stories are true, but locals—including my delivery boy—fear to tread even that road during the day.'

It was only natural that Sonu, Bablu, and Jimmy agreed between themselves that they would not be able to live in that house even for one night longer and would return instead to the hostel.

They swiftly packed their luggage and called for a tempo. As they prepared to leave, Jimmy couldn't resist peering one last time through the grilled window of the room into the backyard.

The bucket and the pulley still dangled over the dry well. As a sudden gust of wind swept through, the copper bucket began to sway, clanging against the well's opposite wall.

Jimmy walked out and joined Sonu and Bablu in the tempo. As the driver started the engine, he looked up. On the first floor, beside the window near the cot, stood a human figure, shaking, and shivering. The paralytic old lady was no longer confined to the bed.

She couldn't be because when Jimmy's eyes turned up towards the terrace, he saw her pacing there, growling to herself, then wailing loudly to anyone who might care to listen.

SNOW BUNNIES

'The snow fell softly; the flakes danced and whirled blanketing the surroundings in a hush, and the timeless play of children, forever etched in the winter light, long after their last breaths warmed those frosted panes.'

The often-gentle winds and calm surfaces of soft snow so emblematic of better times sometimes hide baffling tales and secrets in their currents and crevices. Even the township of Shimla and hamlets all over Himachal Pradesh are full of ghostly whispers. Those who claim to have experienced them, narrate them with such conviction that it is difficult for even sceptics to dismiss these accounts as mere illusions. Perhaps that's where one finds a grey area between the real and the imaginary.

Twenty-eight-year-old Dr Swati Gautam had pondered over certain happenings in this area for over a decade now. She had experienced some strange things personally. She still recalls the incident vividly although it happened about ten years ago.

That winter day was freezing and particularly dark.

Swati was plodding her way through the snow towards the main bus depot in Shimla, where she had to catch a bus to Solan to appear for a competitive exam, at the Horticulture University, her examination centre. Barely out of her teens, she was still weighing different career options in medicine, and was inclined towards psychiatry.

Her predilection for what was purely 'scientific' prevented her from believing in the authenticity of any 'eerie' incidents her friends and acquaintances would relate to her as real-life happenings.

'I was there! I saw it!' they would insist, while trying to give their stories an autobiographical spin.

'What rubbish!' Swati would retort dismissively. 'There's nothing in science to prove that such things could happen.'

She had started the long trek from Sanjauli where she had spent the night before daybreak. It was still dark. As she came closer to town, streetlights appeared to blink at her through the shadows of the deodar trees. She must have walked for about a mile, when at a turn on the road something unusual happened.

The streetlights suddenly went off and the elongated shadows of the trees vanished. What remained visible was a ragged landscape: a few untidy patches of snow and the scary stare of bare branches, reminding her of old men in white with tattered clothing. Some swayed forward, as if in encouragement; others flung her a smile that was more like a snarl, a warning of bad tidings to come.

This fear was completely new to her. 'All illusions... may be hallucinations,' she told herself trying to dispel this uneasy sensation that brought with it, confusion and disbelief. She missed a step on the slushy road and fell. The pain was so excruciating that she feared she had fractured her leg. But she somehow got to her feet and managed to reach the vicinity of the Shimla Government Medical College which lay along her route.

She had barely recovered, when she saw three kids sliding over the now snow-encased slope leading to the college. Their faces were mostly obscured by the swirling white snow and they appeared to be speaking in hushed, indistinct tones. The dark-complexioned children—one of them a girl about three years old—were wearing shabby clothes and torn woollen caps that barely covered their heads. Tiny clumps of cotton wool were plugged into their nostrils and ears.

Swati froze. When she lifted her foot, she could barely walk. She found she was desperately dragging herself away, almost parallel to the ground, away from the new creatures and the strange noises they made to communicate with each other.

She had covered a few yards when she heard other noises. Moving further, she discovered that the sound was coming from a flock of goats and sheep being herded towards the ridge by a man and a woman. Fortunately, her power of reasoning and her rationale returned to her aid and she tried to shake off fears hitherto unknown to her.

Wishing to share her relief, she called out cheerily to the couple: 'You left your kids behind. But never mind. They are playing safely on the slope!'

But her words were met by the most inscrutable expressions judging from the dazed look on the couple's lined faces.

'We have no kids. There is no one out there,' the man said. The couple passed on and the bleating of the goats faded after them.

Swati had reached Lakkar-bazar. It was still some distance away from the bus terminal. By then, the streetlights had lost some of their significance as dawn had arrived.

It took her another fifteen minutes to reach the depot and board the waiting bus. It took her to a stop at the bypass to Solan. From here, she took another bus and walked the rest of the way.

A small distance ahead, she once again heard goats bleating. A goatherd accompanied them. His lined face and dazed expression was startling and she could recall his face immediately. Even before she could ask, the strange smile returned to the man's face.

'They were not children... at least not in flesh and blood... but ghosts. Never mind... they play on their own and do not harm anyone.' And the old man vanished with his flock.

Swati was left dazed, unable to figure out how the old man had travelled with his herd the one-hour distance on foot in such a short span.

Ten years later, Swati had become a practising doctor in a tribal area of Kinnaur, some 250 km from Shimla. On a holiday trip, she went to meet her college mate Kritika, now a scientist researching cures for neonatal deaths. The two friends were taking a nostalgic evening stroll around the campus, which had once housed them and nurtured their ambitions. Swati's eyes fell on a slope that looked oddly familiar. She was convinced that the area had some connection to her past.

Kritika noticed that her friend had stopped stock still and was staring ahead at something only she could see. In a friendly, matter-of-fact way, she slapped Swati's shoulder.

'Till a few decades ago, they would bury dead babies right behind that streetlight—these included babies who were newly born and others who had died of some incurable diseases. But when some residents and passers-by started complaining of seeing the ghosts of those babies in these parts, the hospital authorities decided against burying the bodies here. *Such stupid superstitions!* Do *you* believe in all this rubbish?'

Swati did not answer. She had a blank look on her face.

THE SOBBING GRAVE

'It was just a joke—until he never laughed again.'

Those were the bone-chilling nights of January in the hill town of Kasauli. The students of a Delhi-based school in Dhaula Kuan had arrived for a week-long trekking and adventure camp. After a long day of gruelling hikes, they gathered around the warmth of the campfire, their laughter echoing into the dark forest.

Akaash strummed his guitar, the haunting melody weaving into the crackling of the flames, while others danced and joked. The night seemed alive with energy, masking the ominous stillness of the hills.

As the darkness deepened, the instructor—a retired Subedar from the Army—announced the night trek. The participants scrambled to prepare for the adventure. Akaash tightened the straps of his backpack, gripping his silver torch, and joined the others as they formed a line.

The instructor's voice pierced the crisp air 'It's a narrow and steep climb, with a gorge on one side and thorny bushes on the other. Stay in single file and watch every step. No straying.' The group began their ascent through the dense pine forest. The crunch of their boots on dry leaves and muted chatter occasionally broke the heavy silence. Akaash walked second-to-last in line, with his mischievous classmate Raaj bringing up the rear. They had been classmates since their kindergarten days.

Raaj's antics began almost immediately. Tugging on Akaash's rucksack, he whispered, 'It's the ghost of the hills playing with you, bro. Don't you dare look back!'

'Stop it, Raaj! 'Akaash hissed, irritated. But Raaj continued to tease him. *'Qadam Badhaye Jaa, Khushi Ke Geet Gaye Jaa,'* he began to hum, mimicking their instructor's booming voice. Akaash too soon joined him in mimicking the disciplinarian, who was asking the group to take quick steps.

As the trail grew steeper, the instructor began sharing wilderness survival tips. Akaash, distracted, fiddled with his torch. His rucksack hung loose on one side, and he suspected Raaj's pranks had undone the strap. Frustrated, he muttered, 'Raaj, tighten the left strap of my backpack, will you?'

But there was no response.

'Raaj!' Akaash called, turning around—and froze. Raaj was nowhere to be seen.

His heart pounded as he swung his torch around, its beam cutting through the darkness. The trail behind him was empty. Shadows of gnarled branches stretched like clawed fingers, swaying ominously in the cold wind. Raaj's giggles persisted, like faint echoes in the night.

'Sir! Sir! Raaj is missing!' Akaash's panicked voice echoed like a cry for help swallowed by the dark forest.

The instructor, who was walking a few steps away, looked at him with suspicion and interjected,

'Where can the bugger go in this darkness? No mischief with me or I know how to straighten up you crooks,' said the instructor, still sceptical. 'Everyone! Look around for this boy, Raaj,' he commanded.

The group halted, tension thickening the air. They retraced their steps, calling out for Raaj, their voices trembling. But Raaj was nowhere.

Not even a footprint marked the trail.

'Raaj! Raaj!' they called out, their voices cracking with desperation. Their voices grew hoarse with shouting. The playful curiosity that had accompanied them now curdled to dread. But the instructor was sceptical, suspecting the boy had simply slipped away to return to the camp rather than endure a gruelling night out in the cold forest.

They retraced their steps in a frantic rush, stumbling over roots and loose stones, brushing past the thorny undergrowth that clawed at their clothes.

Back at the base camp, fear clung to the students like a suffocating shroud. Soon the instructor summoned Ram Lal, the elderly caretaker of the camp. Bent with age and carrying a dim, flickering lantern, Ram Lal arrived wearing a grim expression.

Akaash narrated to him what exactly had transpired before he discovered Raaj's disappearance.

'Follow me,' he said in a gravelly voice. 'And don't make a sound.'

The students hesitated but after exchanging anxious glances obeyed as Ram Lal's silent nod urged them forward. He stepped ahead, leading them toward a jagged gorge shrouded in mist. As they approached, the rocky earth gave way to a narrow flight of moss-slicked stairs, old and crumbling, as if resisting the weight of the living.

Each step downward pulled them deeper into shadow. The air turned damp, thick with the scent of wet stone and rotting leaves. Somewhere below, a stream gurgled unseen—but it sounded less like water and more like something breathing.

Then came the sound—faint at first, like a sigh trapped in stone. A low, guttural sobbing echoed up from the depths, chilling but humanlike. It rose and fell like a mourner grieving in the dark. The students froze. Soon a chilling sobbing sound began to echo through the darkness, making the students falter.

Ram Lal approached an ancient oak tree, its twisted, naked branches clawing at the starless sky. Beneath its roots lay a crumbling grave, its surface cracked and hollow. As he raised his lantern, the light revealed a dark opening in the grave. Inside, Raaj sat hunched, his face buried in his hands, trembling as muffled sobs escaped him.

He seemed reluctant to come out. The instructor who flanked Ram Lal carefully pulled away Raaj and offered him some water from his Deoxy Army Water bottle.

'I…I heard someone calling my name,' Raaj stammered, his voice barely audible. 'I followed the voice. It led me here, but then…the voice drowned,' added Raaj who could not stop sobbing, his face gloomy with fear.

Ram Lal's face darkened, his voice low and foreboding. 'This grave belongs to a boy who disappeared in these forests many years ago. His friends—foolish boys—played a prank and abandoned him near the gorge. He cried for them in fear, but they watched him from a distance, hiding themselves behind the bushes. After a while his cries fell silent and when they returned to tell him that they were playing a prank, the boy was gone. They looked for him all around but did not find him. There was no sign of him. His body was never found, but locals believe he drowned in the stream. And now his restless soul roams these woods, calling out to those who ditched him on that fateful day.'

The group shivered. Their fear was palpable as Ram Lal continued with the tale, his voice barely a whisper. 'The villagers built this grave to pacify his spirit, but his soul is still searching for peace.'

Suddenly, a harsh gust of wind extinguished the lantern.

Ram Lal trembled, whispering, 'The boy needs peace.

His body lies somewhere in the gorge.'

The instructor mustered courage and led the group deeper into the wilderness. They searched all night, their torches flickering in the damp shadows, but the forest gave up no secrets. Nobody! No clues! Just that persistent, heart-wrenching wail that seemed to echo from nowhere.

As dawn broke and they trudged back to camp in silence, Akaash made sure to keep Raaj within arm's reach this time. Behind them, walked the instructor and Ram Lal, weary and shaken.

Just as the first light of dawn spilled over the ridges, Raaj froze again.

His breath hitched. His skin blanched. The others turned to him.

And then it came—on the wind.

A voice.

Barely a whisper.

Fragile. Desperate. Undeniably human.

'Hey…help me…please don't leave me alone….'

It came from behind them.

But no one dared turn around.

As others resumed walking, Raaj stopped again, his eyes locked on something in the mist.

'What is it?' Akaash asked.

Raaj didn't speak. His lips moved soundlessly before he whispered, 'That's… not my voice.'

Then came the cry again—'Help me. Don't leave me alone.'

But this time, it echoed from inside Raaj.

And this time, it seemed as if he was not playing a prank.

THE 'BRIDE' AT THE RAILWAY CROSSING

*'She is the last thing you see before the train goes silent—
hair floating, eyes black, dress drifting like smoke.'*

The faint glow of the dashboard illuminated Sandeep's exhausted face as their car wound through the fog-drenched roads of the Kalka-Shimla Highway. Sleepy-eyed and burdened by grief, he glanced at his cousins: Vishal gripping the wheel with rigid focus, and Varun softly snoring in the backseat. A week ago, their lives had been shattered by the sudden death of Sandeep's father. Tonight, they were returning home in Rohru after performing the solemn ritual of immersing his ashes in the Ganga.

The mountain air was biting cold, and the silence was broken only by the rhythmic hum of the engine. They had driven past narrow railway tracks several times, each time seeing them vanish into the darkness like a mirage. But then, as the car rounded a sharp bend, Vishal abruptly slammed the brakes. The car screeched to a halt, jolting Sandeep and Varun awake.

Ahead, a railway barrier stood resolutely closed, faintly illuminated by the headlights. Sandeep frowned.

At this hour? The watch showed it was 12.30 am.

No train was scheduled on this route so late at night. Vishal craned his neck out of the window but saw no one manning the crossing.

He thought of stepping out to see if there was anyone nearby, but the dense fog limited his view. Outside, the world was a velvety black canvas dotted with the faint, distant glimmer of scattered homestead lights, clinging to the descending fog. Soon, with a soft clunk, the barrier rose—seemingly on its own.

'Malfunction, perhaps?' Vishal muttered, easing the car forward.

But before they could pass, the vehicle abruptly came to a halt in the middle of the tracks. The gentle hum of the engine, their constant companion for hours, abruptly died. A sudden, absolute silence descended like a thick blanket, amplifying the chirping of crickets, that moments earlier, had been a mere background murmur.

Then all three caught sight of a figure emerging from the shadows beyond the tracks. Despite the dense fog, they saw a woman approaching them in the ghostly beam of the car's headlight.

She was dressed in a striking red sari, a golden purse slung over her shoulder, her round face marked by a large *bindi*. She moved with slow, unhurried grace towards their car.

But something was horribly wrong.

Her feet were turned backwards.

Sandeep felt the hair on the back of his neck stand on end as the woman drew closer towards the driver side of the vehicle. Her large inviting eyes locked onto his, and a dry unsettling smile appeared on her lips. It was a smile devoid of warmth. She knocked on the window on the driver's side, her bangles clinking eerily in the still night.

'Hello, can you give me a lift?' her voice rang out.

Panic surged through Sandeep and the others as he frantically shouted, 'Don't open the door! She's not human. Look at her turned feet. She's... a *chudail.*'

Vishal froze behind the wheel, as his trembling hands fumbled with the ignition key. Varun, numbed with fear, frantically rummaged through their belongings, trying to retrieve the bottle of holy water. The woman banged harder on the car window, her smile twisting into a grotesque sneer. Her once-beautiful face seemed to dissolve, revealing sunken eyes, decayed flesh, and a skeletal grin that sent a shiver down their spines.

Vishal turned the ignition, once again but the engine sputtered and failed to come to life.

As the woman's skeletal hands pounded harder against the bonnet, the dashboard lights flickered once or twice, before vanishing altogether, plunging the surroundings into deeper gloom. The scent of pine needles and damp earth, earlier a refreshing aroma filtering through the slightly open windows, now felt heavy… almost suffocating.

Vishal desperately turned the key in the ignition; however, the futile attempt yielded nothing but a disheartening click.

Sandeep muttered prayers incoherently, as Varun quickly sprinkled *gangajal* on the dashboard.

Finally, the engine roared to life. Vishal quickly floored the accelerator. The car lurched forward, barrelling straight through the woman. There was no impact—only the chilling sensation of passing through ice-cold air. She vanished as if she had never been there.

The silver-grey car sped away, and Varun whispered the *Hanuman Chaalisa* under his breath. It was not until they reached Shimla that they stopped their car and parked it under a streetlight. But as they looked at the bonnet, there it was—a deep dent, exactly where she had thumped her fists.

Too shaken to continue, they checked into a hotel near Victory Tunnel. Exhaustion overtook them, but sleep offered no solace.

Morning broke with a knock at the door. The waiter's tray rattled as he brought in the tea and switched on the TV.

'Breaking News!' The anchor announced in a steady voice with a gloomy face.

The screen showed a familiar stretch of road near Kandaghat on the Kalka-Shimla Highway. A car stood stalled at a railway crossing, twisted, and charred.

The headline scrolled across the bottom:

'Horror at Rail Crossing: Three found dead in car at the Kalka-Shimla Railway Crossing. Eyewitnesses mention a woman in a red sari was seen moments before the crash.'

The room fell into a suffocating silence.

Sandeep's hand trembled as he set down his cup. No one spoke. The blood drained from their faces.

The description—so precise, so vivid—matched the woman they had seen.

Had they barely escaped?

Was it the holy water that saved them—or had she simply chosen someone else?

The questions remained unspoken, heavy in the still air.

The news and the blaring music that continued revived the sensational and scary moments. Sandeep, Vishal, and Varun watched in silence as a heavy dread hung over them. No one spoke. They were haunted with the memory of the woman in bridal attire...her loud thumping, and her requesting a lift.

The news bulletin ended. A gentle knock echoed at the door—too soft for the hotel staff, too soon for room service.

They turned towards the sound. The wood around the metal lock on the wooden door creaked under the pressure.

No one moved—too scared to lift their tea cups that remained untouched.

THE SNOWMAN WITH A BLACK HAT

'Every snowflake carried a memory, and some were of faces that disappeared into the valley chill'

Snow was falling in a quiet frenzy all over the valley. From the glasshouse of their hilltop guesthouse, Kabir and Meera watched it cover the deodars and pines outside. The weightless flakes, some large and feathery, twirled lazily in the air like ballerinas before softly landing on the burgeoning white carpet. Far away, the majestic Dhauladhar range and the jagged peaks, capped with the layers of fresh snow, seemed to merge seamlessly with the low hanging clouds.

Beyond the serpentine path that wound toward the sleepy village of Dharamkot about eleven kilometres from Dharamshala, the world was gradually disappearing under a soft white shroud.

Inside, warmth clung to the walls like memories. A fireplace crackled, throwing shadows across the rug. They sat side by side, wrapped in shawls, sipping Old Monk from mist-covered glasses.

'Fascinating! isn't it?' Meera whispered.

Kabir nodded. 'And peaceful. Feels like the world's holding its breath.'

She glanced down the hallway.

'I can't wait to see Aarav's face in the morning. He's never seen snow like this.'

Kabir smiled. 'Let's make him a snowman. Right in the middle of the lawn.' 'At midnight?' Meera raised an eyebrow. 'You want frostbite for Christmas?'

He stood up anyway, grabbing his long overcoat.

'Just a quick one. You know how excited he'll be.'

'Don't forget your umbrella, Michelangelo,' she said half-mocking, half-smiling.

But he was already slipping on his gumboots, grabbing the old black umbrella from the corner.

As the door shut behind him, a strange silence settled over the room. Meera's fingers curled tighter around her moist glass.

She walked toward Aarav's room, where their seven-year-old son had fallen asleep waiting for the snowfall that had finally begun late in the night. Gazing at his peaceful face, she gently brushed a stray curl from his forehead.

She was remembering something—a flicker from another winter, long ago.

***

Ten Years Ago

It had not snowed then, but the chill in the Triund forest near Dharamkot had cut straight through their Delhi-born bones. They were fresh out of college—part of a farewell group trekking through the wilderness.

Meera barely knew Kabir back then. He was the quiet one, always sketching something or fiddling with his carving knife. She had pitched a tent near an abandoned stone hut with her friend Naina, while Kabir's tent was a few trees away.

That night, after a dinner of dry biscuits and lukewarm coffee, most of the group was asleep when she heard someone crying—low, unnatural, followed by a growl.

Terrified, she stumbled through the woods and thumped on Kabir's tent.

'Please! Let me in' He unzipped the flap, wide-eyed. She was shaking uncontrollably.

'I think there's someone—or something—out there,' she gasped. 'I tried waking Naina, but she wouldn't budge.'

He wrapped her in an extra blanket and handed her a cup of tea from the thermos, trying to calm her, though he looked on edge himself.

The tent flap suddenly fluttered, and just outside, two amber eyes glowed in the dark. A low, guttural growl followed.

Kabir froze. 'Snow leopard,' he whispered. 'Don't move.'

The creature stepped closer, tongue flicking out.

Kabir slowly grabbed his torch and shone it straight into the beast's eyes. The big cat hissed and slinked into the deodar trees.

Meera gripped his hand, her voice shaking. 'Kabir... look.'

Behind a thick deodar, a figure stood tall and still, draped in a long coat. His wide-brimmed hat had cast his face in shadow. He raised a hand, slowly, and waved.

Kabir peered again, but the space behind the tree was empty.

'You're imagining things; there's no one,' he said.

But then, from the darkness, a deep hoarse voice floated toward Meera.

'Stay inside. Nature is unforgiving and the leopard remembers faces.'

***

Present

Kabir returned half-frozen but triumphant.

'Done,' he said, rubbing his hands off the snow. 'Four feet tall. Perfect posture. All it needs is a pair of glowing eyes.'

'You and your midnight sculptures,' Meera teased, following him to Aarav's room.

He was fast asleep, lips slightly parted, his breathing slow and steady. Meera smiled and gently tucked the blanket snugly around his shoulders.

Kabir pointed to the toy box. 'Grab two blue marbles for the eyes.'

Later, when the wind had died down, Meera slipped outside, bundled in a shawl.

The snowman stood silently beneath the deodar. There was something unsettling about it...it was too symmetrical, too still.

She pressed the marbles into the sockets Kabir had carved. The snowman's blue eyes gleamed sharply, unnaturally. She adjusted the oversized hat on its head and wrapped her own muffler around its neck.

'You're a handsome one,' she whispered, grinning. 'How about a drink?'

The wind gusted.

Then she heard a familiar hoarse voice, low and chilling:

'Keep the boy inside. It remembers children. Nature is unforgiving.'

Meera spun around only to find no one.

She looked back at the snowman.

Its eyes were *moving,* slowly and independently. It's face twitched, ever so slightly.

Her breath caught in her throat as suddenly a shadow stepped out from behind the deodar. Same long coat. Same heavy boots. The black hat was now in his hand.

He spoke softly, but each word echoed.

'Didn't I warn you last time? You came out again?'

Meera stumbled back, slipping on the ice. She turned and ran for the room; her heart was pounding against her ribs.

The door slammed shut behind her.

'Kabir!' she cried. 'Kabir!'

He rushed out of the bedroom, eyes wide. 'What happened?'

'Where's Aarav? Is he inside?'

They raced to his room. The bed was empty. No footprints. No open doors.

'Aarav?' Kabir called, his voice cracking, 'Aarav!'

Outside, the wind picked up again, howling through the trees.

The snow glowed faintly gold in the early light. To Meera, the snowman looked different now: bulkier, taller, its arms more defined, it's face more sculpted. It looked real. And menacing.

Meera stepped closer and froze.

Half-buried in its chest was something small and soft. She pulled it free. A tiny, blue woollen glove, stitched with a cartoon monkey. Aarav's glove.

The snowman's smile had deepened. Its blue eyes shimmered.

Meera fell to her knees in the snow, crying in despair as Kabir tried to hold her.

'No....' From the woods, behind the deodar, the man in the overcoat stood silently. Watching.

He raised one hand slowly and waved with his hat.

'The snow keeps what it's given.'

Then he turned and vanished into the trees. The wind gusted, howling and wailing through the dark forests.

Meera clutched the glove to her chest and collapsed in the snow; Kabir stared helplessly at the moving shadows of the deodars.

The snowman did not move, but his smile and hoarse voice lingered, haunting the night.

THE CREAKING SWING

'The old swing set groaned a lonely tune in the dusk, bearing the weight of two souls, one of them, a memory'

Almost three months had passed since Gori had last walked through the college gates. Life had not paused; it had spun violently off its axis ever since that one, unthinkable day: the day her father never came back.

Mohan Lal, her father, was a humble auto-rickshaw driver, a cheerful, god-fearing man in his early forties with laughter in his eyes and a kind word for everyone. He had left home early that morning, just like always, with three passengers in his rickshaw. By evening, he was gone, swallowed by the roaring, merciless Parvati River near Kasol. The vehicle had skidded off the narrow road and vanished into the gushing waters below. Neither his body nor the auto was ever found.

The river had kept him and with him, a part of Gori.

As she stepped off the bus and began the long walk home, the noise of the Parvati River rushing beside her felt louder than ever: wild, violent, indifferent. Her eyes instinctively scanned the swirling waters, as if they might somehow return her father's smile, the one he wore while pushing her on the creaky swing under the cedar tree in their yard.

'Don't worry, my Gori,' he would whisper, gently steadying the ropes.

'No one will marry you off without your say. But if you ever fall in love, I want to be the first to know.'

'Oh Baba, I'll never fall in love, or get married,' she would laugh, brushing her toes through the grass as the swing sailed higher. I won't go anywhere. I'll always stay with you.'

A gentle smile would appear on Mohan Lal's face, as he watched Gori grip the worn-out ropes of the swing, striving to push herself higher and higher into the sky. Only after her father's passing did Gori realise how safe and secure she had felt in those moments with him, while striving to reach so high.

Now the swing was still. And Gori had stopped laughing.

When she stepped into the lawn and passed the weathered swing, a sudden gust of wind set it creaking, stirring nostalgia and memories of her father. His laughter lingered in the breeze like an unseen presence. But he was nowhere to be seen.

***

At home, a local cop was leaving just as Gori entered through the iron gate. Her grandfather, his shoulders heavier than before, was in the courtyard to see him off, where he met her.

'They've called off the search,' he said quietly.

'Even the disaster response team couldn't find the auto or any of the dead bodies. It's likely they were caught between the rocks deep below. Too dangerous to retrieve,' he said, then paused, looking at her with tired eyes.

'We'll hold the final rites this weekend. It's time to pray for your father's soul… for his peace. You're the eldest now, Gori. Help your mother. There's a lot to do.'

Without looking at him, Gori clutched her books and disappeared into her room. She didn't speak. She didn't cry. She stood at her window, staring through the misty glass at the cedar tree. The weathered swing hung motionless, suspended in time, like everything else since Baba left.

Gori hadn't been the same since the fatal accident. She no longer spoke to her younger brothers, barely interacted with her mother, and hardly responded to anyone at all. Every evening, she sat silently on the swing for hours, her eyes lost in the tangle of the cedar branches overhead.

***

The day of the last rites had arrived.

A *havan kund* was lit in the courtyard. Holy flames

danced, fed by *ghee* and incense, while priests chanted mantras in rhythm with the crackling fire. Relatives and villagers gathered, offering prayers for Mohan Lal's soul.

But Gori refused to come out.

It was her mother, Nirmala, who tenderly coaxed her toward the flames. She had, not so long ago, urged Mohan Lal to seek a groom for Gori.

Gori had always avoided the subject, retreating to the garden or seeking solace on the swing. Her defiant eyes shimmered with unshed tears, stubbornly refusing to let them fall.

Nirmala had never understood her daughter. She, herself, had been married at fourteen: a dutiful wife, a hardworking mother. Her life was rooted in routine and sacrifice. She couldn't fathom why Gori wanted anything different.

'She's not Miss Manali or some movie star,' she would grumble. 'If you don't marry her off now, you'll be feeding her for life.'

To which Mohan Lal would always chuckle and tease, 'If I can feed you and Mangla-Bindo (nodding at their cows), 'I can feed our daughter too, until the right man comes.'

But now he was gone.

And all that was left were his memories, and unanswered prayers.

***

Gori sat by the fire, still and distant, her eyes fixed on the flames. She did not chant. She did not offer *ahuti*. She sat like a shadow of her former self.

From the crowd, Kamla, the wife of a wealthy orchardist, leaned towards Nirmala and whispered, 'Shastriji matched over twenty qualities between Gori and Vicky. He says January's perfect for the engagement.'

Vicky was a loud, flashy boy with an SUV and no depth. Gori couldn't stand the sight of him. He wielded his father's money like a weapon and expected girls to fall at his feet. But to Kamla and Nirmala, he was a golden match.

Gori shouldn't have heard. The fire was loud and the murmur too soft.

And yet something shifted in her.

Her gaze lifted from the *havan* flames and drifted to the creaky swing outside. It was swaying though there was no wind.

Then she spoke, but not in her own voice.

'No one will decide for her. Let this be my final warning!'

The voice was deep, male, firm, and unmistakably not hers.

Silence fell. Even the priest faltered in his chants. Gori's eyes were blank, her body still, but the voice thundered on.

As the gathering exchanged uneasy glances, her grandfather stepped forward, hands outstretched to steady her. But Gori, defiant, shrugged him off and rose.

Without a word, she walked outside, across the lawn, and sat on the rusty swing. Her feet touched the ground once, and the swing moved.

'Listen everyone! Only Gori will choose. Force her, and I shall return,' Mohan Lal's voice reverberated, leaving a chilling echo in its wake. A collective gasp rippled through the courtyard. Heads snapped up and eyes opened wide with disbelief and fear. The words hung in the air, heavy and ominous, shattering the fragile ambience of mourning and remembrance.

What left the crowd stunned was that it was Gori, who was speaking in her father's voice, propelling the swing higher and higher, with repeated jerks of her feet on the grass.

For a while, the priest faltered and his chanting was replaced by a stunned silence. There was panic among the onlookers, who shifted uneasily as an unsettling silence descended, broken only by the creaking noise of the weathered swing.

***

The next day, her grandfather took Gori to a psychiatrist in Kullu. Gori was calm, polite, and even smiling.

'I don't remember anything, Dadaji,' she said softly. 'Just that…I saw Baba. He was sitting with me on the swing, smiling at me.'

The doctor listened, then asked her to wait outside.

'She may be hallucinating,' he told the old man. 'Or it could be a trauma response. Or perhaps she's pretending, using this to escape a marriage she doesn't want.'

But her grandfather remained unconvinced and quiet.

He knew his Mohan's voice too well and he knew Gori would never lie.

***

A new ritual was planned to bring peace to Mohan Lal's restless soul. The priest said the local deity must be invoked. A *gur*, a spiritual medium, was called and the last Sunday of the month was chosen for the ritual.

The procession began with local bands, music, and chants. Gori sat before another fire. At first, she was quiet, but began to grow restless as the priest with his forehead marked with a *tilak* of sandalwood paste chanted mantras in a resonant baritone.

The weathered swing outside began to rock violently. Gori's eyes were fixed on the cedar tree.

A goat was brought in. It bleated wildly, as if it already knew its fate.

Suddenly, Gori looked transformed. Her expression hardened. She stepped forward and seized the trembling goat. The animal's frightened bleats echoed in the silent hall. With inhuman strength, she lifted the terrified creature, its legs flailing in panic, and hurled it into the crowd. Gasps echoed, the air grew heavy and the unease was palpable. All eyes remained fixed on her, waiting for what she would do next.

Gori's voice had changed yet again—it was no longer her own.

'She stays where she is. And no one, no one, will force her again,' the voice thundered. The crowd and even the priests fell silent for a while. Then the *gur* began chanting rapidly.

The priest with deliberate but quick, measured moments, took pinches of the *samagri*, a potent mixture of grains, dried fruits, and fragrant resins, and offered them to the Fire God.

Each offering followed by the rhythmic chanting and the holy chanting of *Swaha w*as a symbolic surrender that carried prayers for the departed soul.

Her mother, weeping, held Gori's arm and led her toward the river.

At the riverbank—the same place Mohan Lal had vanished, the final sacrifice was made. A sword rose, a goat's cry rang once more and then there was silence.

Gori stood nearby. Still. Quiet. Watching.

Something had passed!

***

The next morning, as she tied her *dupatta*, preparing to bathe, her grandfather asked her gently:

'Are you feeling alright, Gori?'

Gori turned, her expression soft.

'What happened yesterday, Dadaji?' she asked. 'Did something…strange happen? I don't remember much. Just… Baba. Smiling at me. On the swing.'

He looked at her for a while and nodded.

'Nothing to worry about, Gori,' he said.

She smiled and walked outside.

Gori's grandfather stood there speechless as she took small steps towards the swing that moved back and forth in a strong gust of wind.

Gori sat down on it. Her feet touched the ground. Slowly, steadily, she began to swing. High above, the wind stirred the leaves.

Above her, the cedar tree stood tall, its bare branches swaying gently in the breeze. The swing creaked softly in the breeze.

REVENGE OF THE HILLS

'Roots coil beneath your feet, watching, waiting... the earth remembers your crime.'

Meenu Tripathi, a solo traveller and vlogger, had ventured to Manali for her latest assignment. She was filming a vlog on the trekking trails and hikes around Sisu Lake, a destination that had gained newfound attention after the construction of the Atal Tunnel. While the enchanting Rohtang Pass had long been the gateway to the Lahaul and Spiti Valleys, the opening of the Atal Tunnel—a marvel of engineering—had transformed lives in both good and troubling ways. Travel had become easier, but the cost was mounting environmental damage.

Meenu was not alone. With her was a group of youngsters from other states, fresh from their trek to the breathtaking Hampta Pass. They lounged by the side of the serene Sisu Lake, soaking in the stillness of the snow-capped mountains around. Families picnicked nearby, enjoying a day of boating and snacks. Children paddled small boats across the clear water, their laughter mingling with the crisp mountain air, while their parents watched from the shore, wrapped in warm jackets.

The peace did not last long. A gang of rowdy youngsters soon shattered it, their SUV thumping with obnoxious music at full volume. They parked carelessly by the lake and burst out, carrying beer cans and tossing litter as if the land was their personal dumping ground. Shirtless in the cold, they danced and guzzled alcohol, a jarring spectacle against the serene backdrop of the mountains.

Amid the chaos, another youngster separate from the group staggered towards a towering Himalayan blue pine. Shabbily dressed and clearly drunk, he clutched a beer can in one hand and muttered under his breath. His staggering steps brought him dangerously close to the ancient tree, its thick trunk radiating silent dignity.

'Be right back!' he slurred, fumbling with the zipper of his trousers. The intent was clear. Around him, murmurs of disapproval spread as onlookers froze in shock and disbelief. This was desecration in its truest form.

Then a deep, gravelly voice cut through the cold air: 'Stop right there! Don't you dare disrespect that sacred tree!'

All heads turned to see a figure emerge through the snow flurries. A rugged motorbike rumbled onto the scene, the sound of its engine blending with the whispering wind. The rider dismounted briskly, his leather jacket creaking as he moved.

The word *"Green Warrior"* was emblazoned in bold but

faded green on the side of his bike, alongside an emblem of interlocked leaves and hills. His jacket bore the scars of rough terrain, and a fresh, bloodied bandage wrapped across his forehead hinted at a recent injury. His steely eyes burned with fury.

'Who are you to stop me?' the drunkard spat, putting up a show of bravado, though his legs wavered. 'It's just a tree. I'm among nature, answering nature's call!'

The man with the blood-soaked bandage strode towards him, boots crunching in the snow. The air, itself, seemed to weigh heavier with each step. 'Disrespect nature and you will pay the price,' he said with a growl. 'These trees are sacred. They protect us. They're not yours to defile!'

The drunkard made a feeble attempt to disregard the warning, but the biker shoved him away from the tree, roughly. The youth crashed into the snow; his beer can rolling away as he landed with a thud. Silence gripped the lakeside. Someone hastily switched off the music. Onlookers watched in awe and trepidation.

Oblivious to the attention, the biker swung his leg over his weathered motorbike. The Royal Enfield Bullet 2000 coated in dust and snow, looked as if it had survived a thousand journeys through tough terrain. He turned the ignition key, and the engine roared to life, its guttural growl reverberating across the valley. Flecks of ice and dirt sprayed as the bike surged forward, disappearing into the swirling snow. Only the echo of its haunting engine and the faint words painted on its side—Green Warrior—remained.

***

As dusk settled, the weather turned ominous. Snowflakes fell thickly, and the group hurriedly boarded their bus. Meenu settled into her window seat, her selfie stick clutched tight, still replaying the surreal encounter in her mind. The drunk, now chastened and silent, slumped into a seat a few rows ahead, muttering incoherently.

The bus began its ascent toward Manali. Inside, the conductor, a young man sporting a multi-coloured Himachali cap, barked instructions: 'No throwing trash out of the windows in the Atal tunnel! And keep your heads inside unless you're tired of living!'

Passing through the Atal Tunnel was a surreal experience, the warm lights casting a strange glow over the icy exteriors of the passing vehicles. But as the bus emerged on the other side, a ferocious snowstorm greeted the passengers. The serpentine descent of the road turned into a nightmare, the vehicle skidding as the driver struggled to maintain control.

Suddenly, the bus slammed against a decaying tree that was leaning onto the road. There was a jarring thud, and the bus teetered dangerously over the cliff's edge. Screams rang out as the passengers scrambled for safety. The vehicle groaned under the strain. The blizzard's howls swallowed their cries for help.

Through the storm came the growl of a motorbike. A biker appeared, jacket torn, gloves streaked with blood, his bandaged head ghostly in the snow light. Without hesitation, he smashed the bus windows with a sense of brutal efficiency and began pulling passengers out to safety. His movements were quick, deliberate, as though this was not his first rescue.

One by one, he saved the passengers. Only the drunken youth was left in the teetering bus. The tree groaned under the weight of the bus, its roots shifting beneath the snow, almost as if rejecting him. Before anyone could reach the youth, the bus lurched violently and plummeted into the abyss.

The storm took a while to clear. A rescue team arrived and tended to the shaken passengers.

Meenu overheard the hushed voices among them. One of them whispered, 'This reminds me of that fatal accident years ago…the Green Warrior.'

Meenu's ears perked up. 'He was an environmental activist,' the man continued. 'He fought tirelessly to protect the forests around these mountains. Rode a Royal Enfield through these valleys. They say he died saving a bus stuck by a cliff, just like this one. They never found his body. Only his wrecked motorbike was found at the bottom of the gorge. That was years ago, but locals still talk about him. Some even believe his spirit roams these hills, watching over them, protecting nature from harm.'

Meenu's heart raced as sudden realisation struck her. The biker who had saved them was no stranger. It was the Green Warrior, long dead but still guarding the mountains he loved. The thought sent chills down her spine as she glanced toward the towering Himalayan Blue Pines and their branches swaying gently despite the devastation.

Far below, the wind whispered through the valley: *Respect the hills, or they will never forgive you.*

THE SHROUD THIEF

'He died with his eyes open, waiting for a kindness that never came.'

The wind whistled through the hills like a mournful hymn, brushing against the moss-stained walls of Shimla Medical College and Hospital. Perched in eerie stillness among the pines, the British-era institution stood like a relic of forgotten dread. Its mortuary, long feared even in hushed campus whispers, had begun to throb with something darker. Beyond the stench of decay and the weight of death, it harboured secrets that refused to stay buried.

As the second wave of Covid-19 ravaged the township, the old building seemed to awaken…not just with bodies, but with unfinished stories.

One day, Abhay Dolta, the mortuary attendant, was jolted awake by frantic banging at his door.

'Come on, Abhay! Make way for another body,' shouted Dr Ronny Victor, head of the forensics department.

Abhay, bleary-eyed, stepped into the corridor. 'Sir, we already have seven bodies lined up. The freezers are full. We've been piling up corpses one after another on stretchers every night.'

The hallway was crowded with the dead. Most had succumbed to Covid complications. The hospital was flooded with patients, collapsing under pressure of the devastating virus. Night after night, seven patients passed away, and the mortuary had become a grim holding station before cremation.

In over a decade of his service, Abhay had never seen anything so horrifying.

'Hurry up, Abhay! More are coming,' Dr Ronny snapped.

'Let me wake Johnny, Sir,' Abhay said, quickly leaving the room.

Johnny was a part-time worker, once helpful during autopsies, but now reduced to prepping bodies for cremation. A habitual drinker, he stayed on mostly for the promise of free liquor and easy work. His real name was Rinku, but everyone called him Johnny, after the famous Hindi film drunkard played by Johnny Walker.

Lately, something strange had begun to happen. For the past week, every morning, one of the white shrouds covering the corpses would go missing.

Johnny dismissed it at first, blaming his drunken stupor. But when it happened again, he was certain.

'Sir,' Johnny muttered one night, 'it's the ghost of the deceased Bishan Thakur from bed number 13. He's taking revenge.'

Thirteen Months Ago

Bed 13 in the ICU had earned a macabre reputation. During the first wave, thirteen patients had died there in barely two weeks. The last one to succumb was Bishan Thakur, a 42-year-old driver from Kotgarh and Johnny's childhood friend.

A chain-smoker since school days, Bishan was rushed to Shimla when his oxygen levels dropped. His teenage daughter, Rashmi, had stayed by his side.

'She's just a kid, and too young to face the harsh realities of life and death,' Bishan had told Johnny in the ICU, his chest wheezing. 'She knows nothing. When I go, make sure all my rituals are done properly, and that I'm wrapped in a white shroud. Be particular, or I'll haunt this place forever.'

Bishan had shown Johnny a small piece of white cloth—a one-by-two-meter shroud tucked beneath his pillow. The sudden spate of quick deaths had caused a shortage of *kafans* and other items needed for the last rites of the deceased and Bishan did not want his daughter to face any difficulties in completing his last rites.

Moments before Bishan breathed his last, Rashmi had rushed to call the doctor in a desperate bid to save him.

When Rashmi returned with the doctor, she found her father's body limp, his mouth agape, and eyes still wide open, staring toward the door. She let out a ragged scream that echoed down the sterile ICU corridors. All

OF GHOSTS, BHALLUS AND A MISSED GOODBYE

- A True Story of Regret and a Lost Friend

It is said that the ghosts of our actions or inactions often linger longer than we anticipate—haunting us with memories, regrets, and what-ifs. I realised it after what happened on the morning of 18 April 2025. That morning taught me one of the harshest lessons of my life. It was the kind of realisation that hits not like a moment of clarity, but like a wave of helplessness—crashing again and again.

Deepan Joshi, my dearest friend and one of the most grounded, empathetic souls I've known, passed away suddenly. A day earlier, I had ignored a call from him. I was upset briefly, because he hadn't taken my call prior to that. I told myself I would call him later. I even planned the exact spot—the slip road at the Kharar underpass leading to the Airport Road in Mohali, where we often spoke during my weekend drive back home from Dharamshala to Chandigarh. But by the time I called, at 6.45 pm, amid crawling traffic, he was already gone.

hell broke loose when she discovered that during her brief absence, the precious *kafan* that her father had hidden under his pillow was gone.

Rashmi whimpered, clutching the empty space and glancing suspiciously towards the corridor, where paramedics were wrapping the body of a patient while relatives stood at a distance waiting to lay the shroud once the hospital staff had finished with the body.

Her father had trusted her while himself preparing for a ritualistic departure well in advance, but now even this last dignity had been stolen from him.

'I failed you Papa...,' his daughter sobbed, crumpling on to the floor beside his stretcher. 'I promised I would take care of everything.'

The nurses tried to pull her away, but she clung to the cold metal frame until they physically lifted her and led her away. All the while, she was wailing at the sight of her father lying there inert on the stretcher.

From that night on, Dr Ronny had noticed something inside Rashmi had cracked—and hardened.

***

Present Day

Now, each night, another corpse was stripped of its shroud. Johnny, haunted by Bishan's warning, was convinced it was his ghost that was lurking in the ICU, seeking revenge.

'Nonsense!' Dr Ronny Victor had quipped dismissively. 'You're drinking too much. We'll install hidden CCTV cameras in the mortuary. No one must know. Tonight, let's monitor the feed and get hold of this bloody thief.'

That night, Doctor Victor, Johnny and Abhay sat in the control room staring at the monitors. Just past midnight, something flickered on the screen.

A lean figure, around five foot five, slipped into the mortuary. It moved quietly to a stretcher, removed the shroud, folded it carefully, and slung it over its shoulder before slipping out.

The face was blurred. Only a long nose and ears were visible before the feed went black.

'See? I told you, Sir. You can't record a ghost,' Johnny whispered.

But Dr Ronny Victor wasn't convinced.

The next night, they waited again. When the figure appeared, Dr Ronny and Abhay rushed after it, trailing it down a forested trail that led to an old British cemetery—now converted into a Covid cremation ground. The wind howled, moonlight filtered through the pine trees, and the air was thick with the scent of damp earth and burning wood.

The figure knelt by a moss-covered pedestal behind a tree. It placed the folded shroud atop the stone and whispered:

'I'm sorry. I couldn't stop it from being stolen. Ever since that night, I haven't slept. This is the 13th night I've come to apologize. I'll keep coming…until you forgive me, Papa.'

The figure slowly removed a mask—a prosthetic, with exaggerated features. Beneath it emerged Rashmi's tear-streaked face. She was smiling and crying at the same time.

'Forgive me, Papa. I couldn't give you the farewell you deserved. But I will make sure none of them rest in peace either. No more *kafans* for those who robbed you.'

Rashmi's eyes were filled with sorrow—and vengeance.

Doctor Ronny and Abhay froze in the shadows.

As they stood there, the night grew colder, the wind sighed louder as it ripped through the trees. They could faintly discern a shimmering figure between the graves—tall, broad-shouldered, watching Rashmi in silence.

The doctor couldn't help but wonder: were the deaths in the ICU following Bishan's passing just a coincidence? Or was it the consequence of a promise unfulfilled, and a daughter's guilt turning into revenge?

The wind howled softly through the pines.

Somewhere in the shadows, a girl in mourning walked again—shroud in hand, guilt on her shoulders, and a sense of justice in her eyes.

And walking a few paces behind her, unseen by all but the trees, was a father—wrapped not in a white cloth, but in sorrow, keeping his vigil until her burden—and his—could finally be laid to rest.

THE HAUNTING SHORTCUT

The air was crisp with the scent of burning lamps as Diwali celebrations were about to begin. Simmi and Binni, two sisters in their early teens, hurried along the winding village paths by the Beas River in Manali. After delivering sweets to their uncle, they had stubbornly decided to take a shortcut home, ignoring his advice to wait for him or to take the safer, longer crowded road back home.

'It's just two kilometres, and we're not kids anymore Uncle,' Binni had said confidently. Simmi nodded, suppressing the sense of creeping unease within her.

The narrow trail they chose cut through ancient apple orchards, long abandoned and half-swallowed by the wild undergrowth. Night had fallen thick and heavy. Far away, on the other side of the river, the faint lights of hillside homes flickered like restless fireflies. Here, though, there was only darkness—and a silence so complete that the crunch of their own footsteps seemed a violation of the peace.

Simmi remembered their mother warning them, 'Never walk past the old orchards after sunset—that land is haunted.' She had always laughed it off during the daytime, even pretending to see ghosts among the trees to annoy her mother. But now, with the weight of night pressing down on them, the words seemed to ring strangely true in her mind.

They had barely walked half a kilometre when something strange happened. Simmi felt a sudden, icy resistance grip her ankles. She glanced down—but there was no mud, no roots, nothing visible. She tried to move faster to keep up with Binni, but her feet grew unbearably heavy, as if unseen hands had latched onto her legs, pulling her down into the earth.

'B-Binni….' Simmi tried to call out, but her voice was just a whisper. Panic clawed at her throat. She staggered forward, but couldn't move more than a few inches. Desperate, she forced out a louder cry, 'BINNI! I CAN'T MOVE!'

Binni, annoyed, didn't even turn around. 'Stop joking, Simmi! I'm not falling for your pranks, tonight!' she snapped, quickening her pace.

Terror surged through Simmi. 'PLEASE, Binni!' she screamed. Her voice, strained and unnatural, seemed to echo around the silent trees.

Something cold brushed against her calf—a touch that did not belong to this world. It wasn't wind. It wasn't her imagination. It was something real.

Binni finally turned—but only halfway. 'Don't look back!' she shouted urgently, her voice trembling now. 'Grab my hand! Quick!'

Simmi lunged forward, clutching at her sister's hand. Together, they stumbled toward the steep stone steps that led to their village. As they climbed, Binni too began to feel an invisible weight on her legs—that same dragging, suffocating pull, like chains binding their bodies.

Shuddering, they began to recite the school prayer under their breath, desperate to fill the eerie silence with something reassuring. The night around them seemed to whisper in return—low murmurs that slithered through the orchard, brushing their ears.

'Why didn't we listen to Mother? We should have heeded Uncle's advice and taken the longer route,' Simmi lamented. But now there was no turning back. It seemed the path behind them had vanished.

Out of the oppressive darkness, a dim light suddenly appeared ahead—the warm flicker of a lantern swinging gently at the crossroads. As they neared it, the terrible weight around their limbs lifted. Gasping and trembling, they stumbled across the village boundary.

Finally, they were home. Safe, but still trembling with fear, Their younger brother Rajan waved at them from the gate, laughing and helping their mother to set up festive lights. Their mother looked up sharply, her smile fading as she saw their tear-stricken, dirt-smeared faces.

'You took that haunted path?' she asked, her voice low and fearful. 'Didn't I tell you never to walk there after sunset?'

'We're sorry, Amma...we'll never do it again,' Simmi whispered, staring at her own feet in disbelief—her slippers were dry, spotlessly clean, as if her feet had never touched mud at all.

Later that night, as they sat huddled near the fire in the lawn, their grandmother quietly told them something after which they never dared to take that shortcut through the naked trees. The orchards they had crossed once covered a burial ground—an ancient one. No matter how many saplings were planted and trees were nurtured, that cursed piece of land could never bear fruit. And on certain nights—nights like Diwali, when the veil between the different worlds was the thinnest—the dead remembered.

And they reached out to haunt those living who had dared to trespass on to their land.

MIRRORS DON'T LIE

'Never again will I trust a smile in the rearview mirror.'

For more than a decade, Nandu Joshi, a seasoned cab driver, had steered his battered Maruti 800 through the winding, treacherous roads of Manali, ferrying tourists, locals, and occasional wanderers with stories to tell. While travelling with him, passengers often spoke of shadowy figures lurking near the cliffs and eerie encounters that sent shivers down their spines. But Nandu would remain unmoved.

Despite the dread that these accounts often instilled, Nandu remained a steadfast sceptic, dismissing them as mere superstitions born of fear.

Superstitions were, to him, the product of lonely nights and restless imaginations, nothing more than fear shaping illusions. That is, until the night he picked up a passenger who changed everything.

That fateful winter evening in December, Nandu finished his last drop-off in the desolate town of Pandoh, some 80 kilometres from Manali. After a quick cup of tea and snacks, he headed back. The sky, a smothering blanket of oppressive blackness, loomed over the silent hills. The thin, high-pitched whistle of the icy wind carried the very chill of the mountains as the biting cold seeped through the cracks of his car's windshield.

As he prepared for his solitary journey towards distant Manali, nestled on the right bank of the quietly flowing Beas River, Nandu's gaze fell upon the small idol of Kali Maa adorning his dashboard. Enshrined in the darkened confines of the vehicle, the goddess seemed to watch him with an inscrutable intensity. Her eyes glinted in the dim dashboard light, unyielding and piercing. The flickering glow barely touched her form, casting jagged shadows that seemed to shift and breathe, as though Kali, herself, had merged with them.

A devout follower, Nandu bowed before the Goddess, chanted her name, and turned the key in the ignition. A deep, shuddering growl split the silence as the engine stirred, sending echoes crawling through the desolate valley.

Soon, he pulled out of town and began the serpentine climb up the winding road after crossing the bridge over the Pandoh Dam, on his way back home. The road stretched before him like a dark, twisted ribbon, its edges obscured by the thickening mist that curled around his ageing 2004 model. On one side, the road hugged the cliffs where workers were carving out a new national highway; and on the other, it barely touched the edges of the mighty Beas, that flowed quietly along, dark, and bottomless.

As he picked up speed on a somewhat wider stretch, Nandu noticed small temple-like structures erected along the roadside. Locals had built these shrines to honour those who had perished in accidents on this perilous stretch alongside the river. These memorials to the deceased were painted in saffron and red, and were believed to offer safety to vehicles, preventing them from plunging into the river below.

Local lore often blamed accidents on a vengeful spirit targeting solitary drivers. Nandu's close friend, also a cab driver, had met a tragic end on a nearby stretch. His car had plunged into a gorge while he was talking to his wife over phone.

The last words the unsuspecting woman heard were her husband's panicked account of seeing a human figure on the road waving at him just before the fatal crash.

Despite his scepticism, Nandu couldn't shake off the feeling of unease as darkness descended and he found himself passing through that very notorious stretch where his friend had lost control. The road was deserted, the darkness unnerving, with overhanging hills on one side and the imposing river on the other.

Feeling uneasy, Nandu stopped at a solitary tea stall for a break. The tea shop owner, a frail and aged man in his seventies, was about to close when Nandu asked for a cup of ginger tea.

'Hanji Maharaj! Aik chai milegi, kadak?' It was a plea with some kind of urgency.

The frail man gave him an unwelcome look, but without a word, he placed the kettle back on the *angeethi* he was about to extinguish.

The man looked up, puzzled but not annoyed. *'Mittha kitna?'*

'Bilkul kam,' Nandu replied, distracted by his phone.

The old man noticed, frowned, and began crushing ginger with a stone.

'Where are you headed, son?'

'Manali, Baba.'

'Be careful,' the old man said, stirring the boiling water. 'There is construction debris along the road and these narrow curves are dangerous. But today's drivers… they can't keep their eyes off their phones. One hand shoots videos, while the other, steers. Then, when things go wrong, they blame spirits.'

Nandu finally looked up. 'So, you don't believe in that ghost story from last week? The driver who crashed after seeing someone on the road?'

The man chuckled grimly. 'Read the paper, *beta*. He was on the phone with his wife. There was no ghost—and he was just a man who didn't see the curve in time.'

The kettle whistled. The old man poured steaming tea into a chipped glass. Nandu drank quickly, grateful for the warmth, but he was shivering, nonetheless.

He banged the glass near the shutter as the old man now closed his shop, and got back into his cab. As he resumed his journey, he placed his phone on silent mode, the old man's words echoing in his mind.

A couple of kilometres later, he spotted a woman standing near a bus stop, waving at him. She was in her mid-thirties, and in traditional attire—a printed *dathu* covering her head, a Kulvi shawl wrapped tightly around her. A worn-out bag hung from her shoulder. Her face carried a weary desperation.

Nandu stopped a few meters ahead. She opened the rear door wordlessly and sat down. A faint scar ran across her forehead and left eye.

'Where do you want to go?' Nandu asked.

'To a village across the river. Just drop me at the next diversion after the tunnel, near the Aut bus stop. I'll find another lift.'

Before he could reply, she added, 'I don't have money. But I need to hurry. My children are waiting.'

There was no request in her voice. Just insistence.

As they drove on, Nandu attempted small talk. 'Where are you coming from?'

She only gave a tight smile.

To distract himself, he turned on his music system. The powerful voice of Narender Chanchal rang out: *'Chalo bulawa aaya hai, Maata ne bulaaya hai.'*

The dashboard idol of Kali Maa glowed orange in the

flickering light. Her eyes seemed even more intense now.

Nandu began humming, seeking comfort in the music.

'Do you mind turning it off, please?' the woman snapped from behind.

Startled, Nandu lowered the volume.

'Not just the noise,' she added harshly. 'That blinking light too. It's too much.'

He switched off the light and glanced back. She sat fidgeting with the scar on her forehead, her face unreadable.

'Do you work nearby?' he asked, forcing his voice to be steady.

'I used to. I was a nurse. But not anymore. Now…I just help people.'

There was a pause.

'Please speed up,' she urged. 'My kids are waiting.'

Nandu increased the speed slightly, even though he knew that it was risky.

As they neared the pitch-black tunnel before Aut, he flicked on the high beams. Yet inside the tunnel, it felt darker than usual—there were no tunnel lights, just his headlights pushing against the thick shadows.

'Isn't it unusually dark here? What happened to the lights?'

There was no answer. He checked the rearview mirror. The backseat was empty.

Confused, he turned to look for her.

She was still there, curled up in a corner, muttering to

herself. His breath seemed to have got caught in his throat. He looked again into the mirror. The back seat was empty.

Then, from the corner of his eye, he saw her smile. A slow, cruel smile and a chill raced down his spine.

The air grew colder inside the car. The engine growled louder. The steering wheel trembled under his grip.

He fumbled to increase the volume.

'Chalo bulawa aaya hai....'

The hymn filled the car, clashing against the oppressive silence.

The dashboard idol flickered violently, bathing the interior in a flickering orange glow.

He could no longer breathe properly. The tunnel seemed never-ending. The car roared ahead until suddenly, there was light. They were out.

Without thinking, Nandu swerved off the road into the courtyard of a roadside temple.

He slumped over the wheel, panting, heart thundering.

When dawn broke, he recounted his story to the temple's caretaker.

'There's a legend,' the old man said. 'A woman died near the river, years ago. She was in a car with her two children. They crashed. She was thrown out and crawled to the roadside, begging for help. No one stopped. She bled to death, and her children drowned.'

He paused, then continued his tale. 'Now she waits on that stretch and hails random drivers. Then, she leads them to a phantom diversion and some never return.'

Nandu was stunned. He thought of her cruel smile. The empty mirror. Her discomfort with the hymn....

A shiver danced down Nandu's back as he realised that the woman in his taxi, demanding and ethereal, was no ordinary passenger. She was a restless spirit, seeking something beyond the veil of death, her presence a harbinger of tragedy on that cursed stretch of road.

He couldn't help but wonder if he had narrowly escaped a fate worse than death, all thanks to the goddess who watched over him from the dashboard, her eyes now solemn and watchful.

As he drove into the welcoming lights of Manali, Nandu glanced once more at the idol on his dashboard. Kali Maa's eyes, still unwavering, seemed to offer both a warning and a blessing, a reminder of the darkness that lurks beyond the veil of the everyday world, and of the silent, watchful presence of the divine that guides and guards the souls who traverse shadowy paths.

Nandu picked up his phone to check the time. A notification blinked on his screen: *Twelve missed calls.*

He hadn't looked at it even once since he had left the tea stall.

Not even when the mysterious woman was there travelling with him in the car.

CORPSE OR CO-PASSENGER? A COMEDY OF HORRORS

'There is no terror in the bang, only in the anticipation of it.'

Tikkam Singh shifted gears endlessly. It was sunset in Shimla. The weather was biting cold and his vehicle—a rickety ambulance that rattled at every turn. Snowy peaks loomed all around and the road twisted and rose with a suddenness that would leave most motorists dizzy.

And to say nothing of the nature of his job....

Tikkam Singh, you see, drove a mortuary van for a living.

That evening, as the ambulance's wheels negotiated twists and turns through a flurry of snow, Tikkam and his companion Heera Lal barely gave a thought to the dead body lying in the back. They were ferrying the body from the Government Medical College in Shimla to the village of the deceased near Mashobra. For the two, it was just another day at work.

If Tikkam's foot pressed a little harder on the accelerator, despite his otherwise controlled driving, it was because he hoped to cover the twenty-kilometre distance quickly, deliver his grim cargo—a victim of a road accident—and return to the beckoning warmth, light and a home-cooked meal before darkness completely swallowed the sky.

The icy winds that whistled through the deodars and bit through the cracks of the windshield almost froze the hand that was changing gears. Tikkam struggled to get the old 1970s model engine up the serpentine road that had unaccountably turned steeper. The speedometer needle sank dangerously close to zero. Tikkam jammed the van into top gear in a desperate bid to negotiate the incline.

In that moment, just as the van staggered before lurching forward again, none of the three passengers—one dead, two alive—realised that they had been joined by a fourth. A man waiting for a bus at a crossing near Dhali, just five kilometres from Shimla, had spotted his chance and leapt quietly into the rear of the van. Pleased with his good fortune, he settled down, smug that he had managed a free ride to his destination.

A rickety partition separated the driver's cabin from the rear of the van. A small grimy glass pane offered only the vaguest view, and no sound carried through.

The steep hike uphill, finally over, Tikkam triumphantly floored the accelerator. In his haste, he had overlooked a speed breaker. The sudden jolt tossed the corpse about. One stiff hand slipped from beneath the sheet and dangled grotesquely before the hitchhiker's horrified gaze. The fluttering white hospital sheet slid away from the corpse's face revealing open, staring eyes and a rictus grin.

The stowaway, who had assumed he was riding with the harmless dead, shrieked in horror. Certain he had stumbled upon a resurrection, he hammered on the small glass pane and shouted, terrified, about resurrected spirits.

Tikkam, now back in full control of his four-wheeler and elated by thoughts of a smoother journey ahead, was blind and deaf to everything behind. Only his companion Heera sitting near the glass panel saw and heard everything.

He clutched at him violently and shrieked, '*Ustaadji! Tikkamji! The body has come alive! He is furious with the living, as you know all these dead people are. He is shouting to let him out! But don't let him! Don't even stop or look back!*'

Tikkam needed no convincing. With eyes looking straight ahead, he drove on like the wind.

The aghast hitchhiker preferred risking broken bones over the vengeance of the dead and hurled himself from the moving vehicle onto the snowy road.

When the pounding on the glass had stopped, a trembling Tikkam and almost hysterical Heera finally slowed, pulled over and crept around to the back. All was calm. The body lay still, only its sheet was displaced and one limb was at an awkward angle. The sinful spark of life had departed again at divine command.

Weak with relief, the two men delivered their burden at the family home—where they were not very happily received—and drove back to their own village, Fagu, left with just enough breath to narrate their harrowing experience to anyone who would listen.

The exaggerations in their story were few, but the words 'devil' and 'god,' 'evil' and 'ghost' entered it frequently.

Heera who had witnessed the thumping by the blurred human image grew animated as he described, 'the spirit that had entered the dead man' and which made him 'wild and aggressive.' The evil in the dead had even tried to stop them at an isolated stretch of the jungle in the darkness, he explained!

But once that deadly stretch had ended, the aggression and the life went out of him again and the dead man lay wrapped in the white sheet looking calm and peaceful.'

The villagers believed every word of the story. They even told the men they were lucky to have escaped as the divine spirits saved them.

Little did they know that just a few kilometres away, in the neighbouring village, "the ghost of the dead man" was nursing his own bruises and vowing to choose his travelling companions more carefully in the future!

The grief was immense. But what hit harder was the ghost of a *Bhallu* that arrived with it.

For years, Deepan and I had a way of coping with life's many shadows—regrets, fears, insecurities. We gave them a name: *Bhallu*. It was our way of making the intangible, visible—the ghosts that followed us, not in sheets or chains, but in thoughts, anxieties, and unsaid words. From career uncertainties to personal heartbreaks, each fear or regret formed the shape of a *Bhallu*: a bear with moods of its own. Sometimes cute, sometimes ferocious, but always around. By imagining them as creatures, they somehow became easier to face.

But this...this *Bhallu* was unlike any other.

This was the *Bhallu* of losing Deepan—without a goodbye. Its claws were sharper than any *Bhallu* before. It haunted not with fear, but with silence—and a deep sense of regret. A silence that hung heavy on every weekend evening, every traffic jam on the underpass road, on every call, I now hesitate to make. It reminded me that I had his number on speed dial, yet didn't answer when he called. That I waited. That I assumed there would be next time. That I took him for granted.

On the morning of 18 April, I woke up feeling unusually proud of my digital detox routine—a new habit of not checking my phone first thing in the morning. But after completing the draft of my last ghost story for this book, when I finally looked, among the routine notifications, there was a message from Shweta, Deepan's wife. Or rather, a message forwarded from her phone.

'With profound grief and deep sorrow, we inform you of the passing of our beloved Deepan Joshi, husband of Shweta Joshi. The last rites will be performed 18.4.2025 at Sector 94, cremation ground, Noida.'

I read it twice. Then three times. My hands began to shake.

I had just spoken to him a fortnight ago for almost an hour on the phone. We spoke of everything—his new walking routine, the irritating fogging in his locality, our usual banter. He even joked about living long enough to see his teenage son Amay settled. 'Billu, we need to live longer,' he had said. 'Even fifteen to twenty more years would be good enough.'

'Kyon Tujhe badi jaldi hai jaane ki? I had laughed.

Then with his usual ease, he had switched to the surprises and performance of an ageing Dhoni in the IPL matches.

Deepan was more than a friend. He was my mirror, my soundboard, my fellow spotter of *Bhallus*. Our friendship had been shaped in small rooms in Paharganj and Sarojini Nagar, refined through shared struggles of journalism, and nurtured through countless conversations that turned even thc mundane into metaphors. We could talk for hours about the rust on a key, the comfort and price of pyjamas from Sarojini Market, or the politics, love lives, and heartbreaks at our workplaces.

Lately our conversations had evolved into a fascinating blend of the profound and the familiar. We dived into the philosophies of Osho, Sadhguru, and Krishnamurti, unravelled their wisdom, questioned their contradictions, and contemplated how their ideas fit—or faltered—within the fabric of everyday life. *Autobiography of a Yogi* sparked reflections that reshaped my understanding of spirituality, forcing me to wrestle with concepts I was only beginning to grasp in my late forties—concepts Deepan had already explored and internalised effortlessly in his twenties.

Then, just as effortlessly, we would shift—seamlessly, like old friends navigating the currents of memory—to the world of Cricket, of the Netflix series that captured the uncertainty and angst of adolescence. In a way that never ceased to amaze me, for he could recall entire dialogues verbatim, delivering them with the same cadence, the same emotions, as if those words had been etched into him, long ago.

It was as though his mind operated on two levels at once—the philosophical and the cinematic—drawing meaning from both, making even the most ordinary conversations feel rich with depth. One moment, he'd be untangling existential dilemmas; the next, he would be quoting a sharp, witty exchange from a show we had watched, bringing it back to life as if it had just aired.

Perhaps it was because he was my roommate—

someone who carried those conversations forward, who lived in the details of dialogue, who understood that meaning wasn't only found in grand philosophies but in the words exchanged between people, in the moments that lingered.... He absorbed wisdom not just from sages but from shared stories, the kind that shaped friendships, shaped perspectives, shaped him.

But we never spoke about how to deal with the loss of a dear friend.

Maybe we believed we would never need to.

He was a gifted storyteller, a natural connector of dots and people. Whether it was an intimidating editor in the newsroom or a stranger in a café, Deepan knew how to slip into someone's world and make them feel understood. It was this gift that made our concept of *Bhallus* so effective. By naming our internal ghosts, we gave them form. And by doing so, we took away some of their power.

But this final *Bhallu* had been relentless. Not just because it came with death, but because it came with silence. With absence. With one missed call.

In one of our last conversations, we had spoken about our parents. Both of us had lost them in recent years. I asked him if he still missed them the way I did, mine. He said, 'Yes, Billu. We all do. But they're around us. You can feel their presence in the little things, in good moments, in unexpected blessings.'

Why we called each other Billu is another story

for another time!

Now, I try to find him in the same way. In the rare hum of a traffic snarl, in a long, aimless conversation, in the rustle of a memory that refuses to go away.

My fellow *Bhallu* spotter left me with the most haunting *Bhallu* of all—the *Bhallu* of a goodbye that never came.

And yet, in the shape of that *Bhallu*, in its fur and silence and unbearable weight, there is a strange comfort. Because it carries his voice, his wit, his love, and our stories. Because even in absence, Deepan has given us something to hold on to.

And because some *Bhallus*, even the heaviest ones, remind us that we once had something so beautiful, its loss could leave a much deeper scar.

Goodbye, my friend. This *Bhallu* is yours. And I will carry it—with pain, yes, but also with gratitude. As *few are lucky enough to have something so precious to part from in the first place.*

The spaces we occupied together will feel different now—quieter, maybe emptier—but they will always carry echoes of you. And when I see that old Bhallu again, worn, and familiar, I will remember us—not just what we were, but what we will always be.

EPILOGUE

WHY DO MOUNTAINS HAUNT?

Locals in the mountains would often warn travellers not to look back while descending from the hills or a pass.

'It's disrespectful,' once whispered an old shepherd to us in Dhancho, a major campsite between Hadsar and Mani Mahesh Lake in Chamba. As his voice rose just above a murmur, his eyes shifted behind us, as though he could already see something. 'The spirits don't like being seen. Not unless they choose it.'

And so, we walked on, resisting the urge to turn. In the stillness of that mountainous dusk, only one sound followed us: the whistling wind. Or perhaps, something walking in it.

Until a couple of decades ago, it didn't matter where you went in Himachal—there would always be a story waiting at the end of a winding road.

These tales were rarely written in books. They passed

from breath to breath, across *chai* stalls, in temple courtyards, beside dying fires. Tales that lingered across mountains and valleys, told in different dialects, wrapped in local backdrops yet sharing the same eerie uneasiness.

They spoke of a British officer, still pacing an abandoned colonial path near Summerhill in Shimla, asking strangers for a matchbox to light a cigarette that never lights. Of a woman in white seen drifting along ridgelines in Kinnaur, never touching the earth, her gaze fixed on another realm. Of footsteps heard in snow at the Rohtang Pass, once an important trade route, but its treacherous terrain and sudden snowstorms made it infamous for being dangerous.

Rohtang La after all, means a 'pile of corpses' in Tibetan. Folklores of lonely women sobbing by the sides of streams, seeking help, or humming lullabies in abandoned hill state castles are just as common.

From the apple orchards to high mountain deserts, from tea gardens to prayer-flagged passes, these legends ripple quietly through Himachal's many regions. A flickering lantern glimpsed in a forest. A masked dancer at a monastery festival who vanishes before the last drumbeat. A phantom carriage that never arrives, yet always departs to the fading sound of hooves. I have heard them all since childhood.

And after years of listening to such ghost tales in creaky wooden homes, around campfires and in smoky cafés tucked in misty valleys, I have realised one thing:

In the mountains, everything echoes—stories, footsteps, even the memories of the dead.

As I bring these tales to a close, from the forgotten corridors of Shimla, once the British Capital, to the lonely trails of Dharamkot; from haunted home stays and rest houses in Kullu and Banjar Valley to cursed railway crossings and bus stops around Kasauli, I return to a question I've carried all along:

Why have the hills always been so haunted?

Mountains have always been more than geography. They are thresholds, sacred in nearly every culture, feared in equal measure.

Here in the Himalayas, areas around it are known as Dev Bhumi—the land of the gods and goddesses. Not only because of the temples clinging to cliff edges or the myths rising with the mist, but because here the veil between worlds feels thinner.

But it is not just here in Himachal.

Travel beyond the Himalayas and you find the same patterns: mountains that remember, forests that murmur, valleys that hold onto voices long after the bodies are gone. The forms and folklore may shift, but something in the altitude seems to cradle the unexplained.

It cannot be a strange coincidence that what the people of Himachal whisper under their breath on foggy winter nights, others halfway across the world, whisper too. The names change, the gods differ, the accents shift—but the stories? They remain eerily familiar.

In the Andes, the mountains of South America, where the air is thin and the clouds kiss the earth, the Incas once carried their children up to the peaks, wrapped in ceremonial cloth, and left them as offerings to their gods. Centuries later, these frozen children, were found perfectly preserved—knees drawn to chest, faces peaceful, as if still dreaming. Even today, five hundred years later, locals still speak of their spirits as protectors, or mourners, depending on who you ask.

In the Scottish Highlands, the landscape is all moor and mist, cut by rivers that run cold and fast. The Valley of Glencoe is steeped in both natural beauty and historical bloodshed. Over three hundred years ago, soldiers from Earl of Argyll's Regiment of Foot massacred several members of the Clan of MacDonald in their sleep. Hikers say the valley still echoes with their cries. They speak of unseen eyes and of music carried faintly on the wind, of bagpipes played by no living hands.

In Japan, at the foot of Mount Fuji, the Aokigahara Forest, that grew on a hardened lava flow from a major eruption of Mount Fuji in 864 CE, stretches wide—a lush green stillness that swallows sound.

Known as Jukai, the Sea of Trees, or more infamously, the Suicide Forest, it is notorious for its eerie silence and dense, disorienting landscape. Legends tell of vengeful Yūrei, tormented spirits of those elderly and sick abandoned through the practise of *ubasute* or of suicides where restless souls still wander and lure others deeper into the forest's unsettling embrace. Compasses falter here, trails vanish, and locals believe the trees themselves hold sorrow with the lingering of the spirits of the departed.

It's a place where the veil between worlds is thin, and the spirits of the deceased are ever present.

And then there's Russia's Dyatlov Pass, where nine trekkers died in 1959 under circumstances that still baffle investigators. Their tents were ripped open from within. Their bodies lay scattered, some without clothes despite the freezing temperatures. Avalanche, military tests, or was it something else out there that night? Whatever it was, it remains something that the mountain never revealed.

It is as though every range on earth sings a different verse of the same ancient song. Each peak is a sentinel. Each story a whisper carried by the wind.

Science has its own explanations behind these stories validating the phenomena in the process. At high altitudes, the brain starved of oxygen, sees things, senses presences, hears voices and invents companions. Mountaineers call it The Third Man Syndrome—that feeling of being followed, accompanied, watched, even when alone.

Then there's infrasound: low-frequency vibrations created by wind funnelled through narrow valleys or hollow rock formations. We cannot hear it, but we feel it—as a pressure in the chest, dread in the gut, the sense that something is wrong, even when all is still.

Maybe that is all that ghosts are—our minds warning us in the language of story.

Then, why do we keep listening?

Because deep down, some part of us wants to believe. Not always in spirits. But in memory. In presence. In the idea that places, like people, remember.

So, like around the world, in Himachal too, hill folk want to believe that the hills hold on to the laughter, the grief, the footsteps of those who came before us. That the deodars of Jibhi in Banjar Valley still hum the songs sung to lost lovers. That the snow of Rohtang carries the secrets of trekkers who never returned. That abandoned houses in Shimla still wait for their last residents to come back.

And maybe, in that belief, we find comfort.

Nevertheless, these ghost stories are not really about fear. They are about connection—to land, to legacy, to loss. They remind us that something always lingers. That some doors never close. That some trails never end.

So, if you ever find yourself alone on a Himachali ridge, and the wind suddenly pauses, and the trees fall still, and you feel the air shift just slightly—Do not be afraid.

It might not be a ghost. It may simply be the mountain remembering or making its presence felt.

THE END

Dear readers, as I end this book filled with tales of ghosts that roam the hills and the horrors that echo in lonely places, I leave you with the truest haunting of all—not the spirits that lurk in forests or ruins, but the ghosts that live within us, born of love, memory, and all the goodbyes we never got to say.